WHO IS MARY WINTER?

WHO IS MARY WINTER?

PAT THORNBOROUGH

WORCESTERSHIRE COUNTY COUNCIL
CULTURAL SERVICES

THORNDIKE
CHIVERS

LIBRARY OF CONGRESS CATALOGING-IN-PUBLICATION DATA

Thornborough, Pat.
  Who is Mary Winter? / by Pat Thornborough.
    p. cm. — (Thorndike Press large print clean reads)
  ISBN-13: 978-1-4104-2055-8 (alk. paper)
  ISBN-10: 1-4104-2055-8 (alk. paper)
  1. Nuns—Fiction. 2. Large type books. I. Title.
PR6120.H669W47 2009
823'.92—dc22
                                          2009026721

BRITISH LIBRARY CATALOGUING-IN-PUBLICATION DATA AVAILABLE

Published in 2009 in the U.S. by arrangement with Robert Hale Limited.
Published in 2010 in the U.K. by arrangement with Robert Hale Limited.

U.K. Hardcover: 978 1 408 45690 3 (Chivers Large Print)
U.K. Softcover: 978 1 408 45691 0 (Camden Large Print)

For Peter

CHAPTER ONE

Sisters — the time has come for us to consider the unthinkable. Yesterday morning I received a letter from — How was she — Sister Joan, Mother Superior of the Stella Maris Convent — going to break the news to her nuns? They had a right to know, and yet what a devastating blow it would be to them. The fact was that she had received an ultimatum from the Mother House to the effect that if their debts could not be paid and the convent fell into even more disrepair, they would be recalled, the house closed, shuttered and eventually sold. It would mean the end of a hundred years of their Order's residence there and worst of all — failure. She decided to keep the letter hidden and the bad news in her heart for a little while longer.

She watched their mechanic close the bonnet of the old Ford in the barn which was attached to the manor house that was home to seven nuns and herself. Manor sounded grand but the old house was only just big enough for them with a spare room for the unexpected guest.

'I've done the best I can, maybe she'll last long enough to get over the next hurdle but I can't guarantee that this old lady will be awarded an MOT next year. I suggest we hope for a miracle to get her over the one she's got to go through this afternoon.' Sister Imelda shook her head and wiped the grease from her hands on a rag that only served to distribute more of the same over a larger area, finishing the job on the skirt of the sacking apron that protected her grey habit. She patted the car gently. 'She's given us good service has this old girl!'

Sister Joan looked at the worse-for-wear car and sighed. The paintwork had bloomed and the Ford logo had lost its lustre. 'There's no doubt about it, she's just an old bucket of bolts,' she said. 'But — she'll just have to make it for another year. We can't possibly afford another one what with all the bills to pay and there's poor Sister Flora, I have to be able to take her to the dentist again on Monday. That tooth will have to come out I'm afraid, it's so wobbly. If we don't get an MOT — I just don't know what we're going to do.'

'You could take a chance that PC Bradley would let you off because you're a holy nun — that's if he catches you — or beg a lift from Mr Murray up at the farm. He's a kind man — wouldn't let a lady suffer. He's helped us before.'

'I know he has. He wouldn't say no even if he wanted to, but we've asked him for so much already, I don't want to be a burden, nor do I want to rub our policeman up the wrong way and it won't really solve the problem will it? We need another car — and soon.'

'Don't say that — she'll hear you.' Sister Imelda grinned. 'Let's just hope for that miracle then wait and see. If we get an MOT then we have a whole year to worry about what to do next.' She took off her apron and removed a large purple anorak from a nail in the wall and put it on over her grey skirt, white winter-warm blouse and cardigan.

'You've done a fine job, sister. What would we do without you?' Joan opened the door and they both went out into the dull morning. 'Hard to believe it's nearly Christmas.' She rubbed her gloved hands together. 'There's a real chill in the air today — rain is forecast for later. Probably just when I have to go to the garage with "Sister Ford".'

They both chuckled at the pet name the nuns had given to their car.

'First of November today — can't get any warmer now until spring.' Sister Imelda pulled the hood of her jumble sale anorak over her head and clutched the edges of the jacket around her ample figure.

As they walked together from the barn to the old manor house, Sister Joan remembered the time their mechanic first came to the convent. It was just such a day as this. She had gone to the station to meet her, some miles from the house. Sister Imelda had got off the train with one small backpack and a large wooden box containing what she called her fixings, which — although it was fitted with small castors on the base — had to be manhandled into the car by an unwilling porter who didn't think he should be doing this in his tea break. He smiled grudgingly and with a look of disbelief when they assured him that God would bless him for helping. Thank goodness for the fixings because the car had broken down on the way back and to Joan's surprise the new nun had the bonnet up, the fixings box open and was up to her elbows in no time. The old car responded like a patient under the healing hands of a surgeon.

'Funny way to follow a vocation, isn't it?'

she had grinned as she closed the bonnet again. 'But I've come in handy all over the place.'

Times have changed, thought Joan. Their habits had altered some years ago from the starched discomfort of the old head-dress and black floor-length robe, to the washable grey skirt, blouse and cardigan, with just a whisper of a grey veil fixed to and held on by an Alice band. The skirt was calf length and much more comfortable for driving and working around the convent.

She smiled across at Sister Imelda who was clutching the purple anorak closer around herself against the chill wind. A purple anorak. Who would have thought it — being allowed to wear such a garment? Hardly ever did the other nuns call her by her title, Reverend Mother: they were all Sisters now. The driving force of their vocation, however, bonded them together and remained as strong as ever.

'Here we are.' Sister Imelda pushed open the heavy front door for her superior. 'Hot tea — lovely — and do I smell scones?'

The warmth of the big hall cloaked them like a blanket as they took off their outdoor clothes and made their way to the heart of the home, the kitchen, where Sister Clare, who managed their domestic life, was setting out mugs and plates for the morning break.

Joan made a mental note to turn down the heating just a little, the fuel bills had been extra large last time. Money was certainly a big worry. They had a living allowance from the Mother House, but they were so few and the Order so small that it didn't amount to much and they were expected to supplement it. The nuns did their best, cultivating the garden and selling vegetables and fruit in season, but the work was hard and it seemed that they couldn't grow enough to meet demand with the few sisters who had been assigned to the task. They took in sewing jobs, curtains, cushion covers and odds and ends. They recited the prayers of their office daily and met in the chapel at set times. Their visits to the sick filled in those times when the social services left a gap and a need in those just wanting to talk. They were the Stella Maris Sisters, their vocation — to pray for wanderers and lost souls in life anywhere they may be and to take in those who needed a roof and a meal.

The convent was quite remote and cars usually kept to the main road which was a few miles along the narrow lane at the end of which was their old house. So, in fact, they hadn't had a wanderer for years, except, Joan recalled, some people last year who wanted a bed and breakfast holiday because the sea was at the bottom of the convent land. She had to refuse because they weren't exactly in dire need, what with the huge Range Rover and the expensive watches — and suppose she let them have the room and then a real wanderer turned up? So she suggested the public house in the village a few miles away who did bed and breakfast. Still, the nuns kept the room always fresh and ready, and food for just one genuine and needy traveller. After that the idea of doing B&B churned around in her mind for days. Times change all the time, she thought, and maybe we should change with them.

Sister Imelda worked very hard, sometimes late into the evening, mending lawnmowers for local people as well as keeping their own old car and rotavator in working order. Joan smiled to herself as she remembered the latter arriving on the back of a truck in a state of rusting antiquity, a gift from Mr Murray who worked the farm next to their land and whom they regarded as their next door neighbour. Sister Imelda nursed it back to health and it gave great help to the gardening nuns — as well as a bill for petrol. The addition of Imelda to the house brought about a change to their income. She was a dab hand at repairing most things so they seldom had to call out a man to fix the old radiators when they got noisy and needed draining. But there was never enough money and they had to rob Peter to pay Paul for most of the year. A small legacy had helped them through last winter, but this year the cold weather loomed as large as the repair bill for the old boiler.

'This one's got me beaten this time!' Imelda had sighed, placing her spanner back in the fixings box. 'I'm afraid this is a job for a professional!' She said it as if the word was spelled with pound signs.

'Here you are, Sisters — nice mug of tea. Two sugars for you, Imelda,' Sister Clare greeted them.

'Oh lovely — just what the doctor ordered.' Imelda sighed gratefully.

Their voices brought Joan back to reality. She took a mug from the tray on the table. 'Scones too, Sister Clare — you're spoiling us,' she said, looking around at them all. The news in the letter that she was hiding weighed heavily in her heart. She couldn't tell them — not just yet.

Sister Clare smiled. 'It's blowing up so

cold, I thought you'd need a little sustenance — it's three hours till soup at lunchtime. How's Sister Ford? Any better?'

'As well as can be expected.' Imelda took a sip of tea and put the mug down on the table. She picked up a buttered scone, completely oblivious to the large dabs of engine oil she had deposited on the side of the mug. 'Just might make it for another year. We can only hope. She goes in this afternoon.'

'Three o'clock — that's when I have to take her to the garage.' The tea was hot and Joan blew across the top of the mug before she drank.

'We'll all say a prayer for her,' Sister Flora said, biting her scone neatly on the side opposite the wobbly tooth.

'Never mind, Flora.' Imelda patted her on the shoulder. 'We'll get you to the dentist somehow, whatever happens.'

Joan saw that their mechanic's fingers were black with grease. She said nothing. Sister Imelda would scrub them soon and those hands worked so hard they'd earned the right to be a little grubby.

Before lunch, as was their routine, they all went to chapel for prayers. They sang the chosen hymns for the day and Joan sighed as their voices rose in unison. They sounded

15

so sweet but — oh, for some harmony. They never seemed to be able to get it right and so Sister Emma who played the small harmonium and was responsible for their music, had quietly given up trying to teach them. There was not much time for practice anyway, what with the weeding and the planting and so on, and so on.

Joan noticed that Emma's hands were dry and rough with the work she had to do and her nails were cracked, but she still played beautifully and never complained.

Hail Queen of heaven the ocean star,
Guide of the wanderer here below. . . .

It was their special hymn. It would have been so nice to do it justice. Joan sent up a silent prayer — please send us an MOT, enough money to mend the boiler and a bit over for the roof. It's so hard to pray with a clear mind and without having to ask for something all the time.

At two-fifteen Sister Joan climbed into the old car, clicked on her seat belt and turned the key in the ignition. The motor sprang into life without a single hiccup. As she moved away from the convent and up the drive to the lane she could see, in her rear view mirror, Sister Imelda standing on the

16

steps of the old house, watching her, with both thumbs up.

The weather forecast had been right. It began to rain as she went through the ever-open iron gates at the top of the drive. She held her breath as she turned on the windscreen wipers — they started, thank heaven. The car was behaving very well indeed having responded to Sister Imelda's tender loving care; in fact it seemed perfect except for the irritating problem with the clutch from time to time. Maybe it was nothing to worry about. Let's hope that Len Harvey at the garage will think the same, she thought, as she turned into the lane. It wasn't as if they used the car for long journeys, just to the village and back mostly and sometimes into town. She thought of the dental appointment on Monday.

'Just one more time, old girl!' she said aloud. 'One more MOT and I promise you'll get VIP treatment for the rest of the year!'

CHAPTER TWO

'Afternoon, Reverend Mother, you're nice and early.' Len Harvey was out on the forecourt when she arrived, holding a large umbrella over his baseball cap and blue overalls. He changed the price on a second-hand car for a lower one. 'Bring the old girl into the workshop out of the rain and I'll do the test for you.'

She drove carefully through the big double doors followed by Len. Furling his umbrella he turned to the boy who fetched and carried.

'Make the Reverend a nice cup of tea, lad — I'm sure she could do with one and so could I.'

'Yes, Mr Harvey. Can I have one too?'

'O'course you can lad — after you've made one for us and checked that all the technology is ready for the test.' He winked at Sister Joan. 'He's learnin' the business, Reverend.'

'I hope you won't be too hard on him Len, nor on our old car.'

'Ahh! I'll do my level best for you within the laws, ma'am. No more I can't do. You go sit in the office while I'm at it; no point in standing around here in the draught. The lad will bring your tea and I'll be as fast as I can.'

'That's kind of you Len, thank you.' She got out of the car, made her way to the tiny office at the far end of the workshop, opened the door and went inside. It was warm and cosy with a desk piled high with paperwork that almost obliterated the computer with which Len had been trying to get to grips since this time last year. Beside it was a comfortable chair, so she sat down and cleared a small space to put the tea when it came.

The lad knocked on the door before he opened it. 'Nice drink of tea, Reverend. Didn't know if you has sugar or not so I put in two spoonsful. If you don't take sugar just don't stir it, OK?' He handed to her nervously what was obviously their best cup and saucer with a rather stained spoon.

'That's very nice, thank you,' she said.

It was a white lie — she'd never taken sugar but the lad was so bright-eyed and eager to please that she didn't have the heart to disappoint him. He watched as she took a sip. 'My goodness, you certainly know how to make a good cup of tea,' she smiled.

He blushed. 'First thing Mr Harvey taught me. He says it's very important to know how to make a decent cuppa!'

'How right he is,' replied Joan.

The lad backed out of the door as if she were royalty and closed it quietly behind him. She could hear voices and the sound of a spanner being dropped on the concrete floor. Looking around her she discovered a little washbasin in one corner of the room and poured what remained of the tea into it, swilling away the evidence with fresh water. Maybe I should drink it, she thought, they were so kind to have made it for me, but I don't like sugar and I'm afraid I'm not martyr material. She sat listening to the rain beating down on the corrugated iron roof.

After a while the door opened again and this time Len came in, a sheet of paper in his hand. His face was glum and she feared the worst.

'Bad news I'm afraid, Reverend.'

'Oh no!'

'She can't make it this time. The repairs we would have to do would cost more than the old girl is worth. Your clutch is almost shot and you're going to need four new tyres. Your rear nearside is almost bald, and your bodywork is full of rust. I'm sorry.' He looked at her with guilt in his eyes as if he were responsible for the blow he had dealt her.

'Oh, it's not your fault, Len.' She clasped her hands together. 'It's just — it's just that she was going quite well on the way here. Sister Imelda has worked so hard and so long — we just needed another few months — then something else might have turned up. I had such high hopes that she just might be able to scrape through.'

'Your mechanic up at the convent is a very talented lady — and if you don't mind my saying — I wouldn't mind her working for me, but the problems are such that even she wouldn't be able to cope. Major work, I'm afraid. Your Sister 'Spanner' has done wonders but it won't last. Can't let the old car through this time — sorry.'

Sister Joan got up from the chair. 'But how am I to get home? I can't drive her now, can I?' She felt tears stinging the back of her eyes. How, oh how, was she going to tell the other nuns and what about poor Sister Flora and her wobbly tooth?

'I was going to tax the car when I went to town on Monday,' she sighed.

'Look here,' said Len, handing her the keys. You've got two more days before you have to tax her so it's OK to drive her home. Limp her along slow and careful; there won't be much on the road on a night like this and you've got to get her back. It ain't right I know, with that bald tyre, but you got her here with no mishap and if you're careful she'll get you home safe. But on no account take her out again even though you've got two days legal — no matter what your mechanic can do! That's the best advice I can give you.'

'I — we'd all hoped for a miracle to get her through,' Joan said wistfully.

'Take more'n a miracle, Reverend — much more'n a miracle.'

The lad's head appeared around the open door. 'Yeah!' he agreed.

Len accompanied her into the workshop where Sister Ford stood. 'How much do I owe you, Len?' She reached for the purse in her coat pocket.

He blushed. 'Oh, that's OK, Reverend — have this one on the house. Save the money towards another car, eh?'

Thanking him, she said, 'Bless you, Len.'

He opened the door for her and she climbed into the driving seat. Even that had a sag in it that she had hardly noticed before. 'Maybe it's for the best,' she said. 'Perhaps something better is coming for us.'

'That's the spirit, Reverend.' Len clicked the door shut and spoke to her through the window. 'We'll look out for a nice little run-around for you, somethin's bound to turn up soon. I'll do you a good price.'

'Whatever it was, we wouldn't be able to afford it,' she smiled sadly.

'Now, now, Reverend — where's that faith and indomitable spirit? Chin up, it'll all turn out OK, you see if it don't. Safe journey now — don't rush it.'

It was dark outside. Joan wound up the window, backed out of the garage and onto the forecourt, into the rain that seemed to be falling even more heavily than when she had arrived.

'Don't worry,' he'd said. The memory of that letter hidden in the drawer of her desk took over her immediate thoughts and she shivered a little as she pulled on her woollen gloves. Tears ran down her cheeks as she switched on the lights and windscreen wipers. I had expected too much, she thought. I took it completely for granted that Sister Ford would pass. As she pulled out into the road she dashed the tears away on the sleeve of her coat. 'Lord!' she said aloud, 'I won't be beaten. You'll do something — I know

You will — but, oh please — do it soon!'

She drove carefully, aware now of the faults that could cause her to come to grief along the lonely road home. The Sisters would be waiting, eager to celebrate Sister Ford's triumph over the world of technology, sure in their faith that there would be no reason for their prayers not to be answered. The rain became so heavy that the wipers were almost useless and she slowed down to a crawl. No other traffic passed her on the main road. She turned into the lane that, two miles further on, would end at the open iron gates and the driveway of the Stella Maris Convent. So intent was she on driving carefully that she had passed the car that stood on the grass verge before she realized that it had no reason to be there at all. The only traffic on this lane was always destined for the convent.

Bringing Sister Ford to a halt, she put her into reverse and backed to where the other car stood in the rain. She wound down her window to see if there was a driver. The seat in the other car appeared to be empty, nevertheless she opened her door and climbed out to look inside just in case the driver had slumped over into the other seat. The rain beat down on her, making her veil cling to her head. The wet folds of it stuck to her face, she pulled it off and stuffed it into the pocket of her coat. She felt the cold discomfort of water trickling down the back of her neck. The darkness smelled of winter and soaked earth.

The car was completely vacant except for a small holdall on the floor of the passenger side. She straightened up and tried to peer through the rain to see if someone might be walking — there was no one in sight. But surely they would have stayed with the car in this weather? Most people had those mobile phones anyway, to call for help. Why was the car here? There was nowhere to go except the convent and they weren't expecting anyone to call. Not even a bona fide wanderer would venture out on a night like this — not these days. A small sign at the top of the lane indicated that only the manor house was at the end and that there was no way through. One of the sisters had made a sign that just said 'Stella Maris' to aid delivery people, but everyone in the village and town knew they were there anyway. Joan was not fond of puzzles and was not enamoured of standing in the rain trying to work one out. She could feel the rain coming through the seams in her coat and soaking into her cardigan.

Shivering, she wiped the rain from her face with her gloved hand then, turning, she got back into Sister Ford, peeled off her wet gloves, threw them onto the passenger seat and started the motor. She drove slowly and carefully along the lane with the rain flowing in sheets down the windscreen. It was hard to see if anyone was walking on the grass verge. Maybe whoever it was had reached the convent already.

It was only a sudden lull in the downpour that enabled her to stop in time before she ran over what looked like a bundle of rags in the middle of the lane. She opened the door and climbed out. Oblivious to the mud and puddles that soaked her feet and ankles she ran over to the spot. It was a girl, lying on her face and wearing only a T-shirt and blue jeans. One foot was bare and the other had on a strappy high heeled sandal. Joan called to her but she didn't move. She was covered in mud and soaked to the skin. Joan fell on her knees beside the girl, turned her over, lifted her into a sitting position and cradled her in her arms. She seemed chilled to the bone. Joan could feel the cold skin of her cheek as she held her close.

'Please, please don't be dead!' She brushed the girl's blonde wet hair away from her face. She was so very young, couldn't be more than eighteen, she thought.

She knelt in the mud of the lane in the beating rain and rocked the girl in her arms. 'Oh, wake up — please, please. . . .'

The girl coughed and then spluttered. 'My car — it won't go — I can't get any further. Must go away — far away as I can.' She looked up at Joan. 'I can't walk any more — so tired — so cold. . . .' She began to tremble and whispered almost inaudibly, 'I don't know who you are. . . .'

'I'm the Mother — I'm Joan — just Joan, don't be afraid. Do you think you can stand up? If we can get to my car I'll take you home.'

'No! Not home — must get far away.' The girl began to struggle to get to her feet.

'To my home, child, I'll take you to my home. You'll be safe and warm there. You can't go any further on your own.' She managed to get the girl to her feet and together they struggled through the rain and the mud to where Sister Ford stood with her lights shimmering through the wet, lighting the way. Joan helped the girl into the back seat where she lay shivering.

Her own hands were shaking as she turned the key in the ignition. The engine wheezed.

'Oh, no — don't play up on me now!' she

27

beat the steering wheel with her wet hands. 'Just one more mile, Sister — just one more mile!'

She felt soaked to the bone, her feet were making muddy puddles on the floor and water filled the sag in the seat. She tried the key again and the engine stuttered into life. 'Thank God!' she said aloud. She glanced back at the girl before she put the car into gear and started off. She was very still. Disregarding Len Harvey's advice about taking it easy she put her foot down and Sister Ford, her back wheels spinning in the mud, plunged forward into the darkness.

CHAPTER THREE

The sisters had put on the outside light so that she could see her way up the drive on her return. It was more welcome than she had ever imagined it could be as she turned in at the iron gates. The nuns must have heard her because the door opened at her approach and they came out onto the step which was sheltered by an arch. It was a bizarre sight under the circumstances, but how could they have known what had happened? One of the Sisters had made a large sign out of one side of a cardboard box and had mounted it on a broomstick. It read, 'CONGRATULATIONS — WELL DONE SISTER FORD' — so sure were they that all was well and that they had their precious car for another year.

Sister Imelda ran forward with a large striped golf umbrella (another bargain from a jumble sale). 'Terrible weather — thought you might need this — Why, Mother, whatever is the matter? What's happened?'

The fact that she used her Superior's official title made Joan realize how dreadful she must look and how concerned Imelda was. She opened her door.

'Put down that umbrella and give me some help, Sister, please! We have an emergency on our hands.' She indicated the back seat.

Sister Imelda glanced inside then gave a longer look. 'Oh my! Oh my! What have you got there?' She opened the back door. 'It's a girl! What on earth —'

'Just give me a hand to get her inside — never mind the rain — just help me lift her. She's desperately cold and she hasn't made a move in the last mile.'

Together they managed to get the girl out of the car. When the other Sisters saw what was happening they too ran to help, regardless of the cold and wet.

'Where did you find her?'

'Do you know who she is?'

'She's cold as death, poor child!'

They put her down on the large rug that covered most of the floor in the hall and Sister Flora closed the front door against the winter night.

'Can she stand?' Sister Emma rubbed the girl's hands. 'We'd best take her to the kitchen quickly — it's warmer in there.'

'Get those wet things off her at once.' Sister Clare had hurried to the airing cupboard and was already back again unfolding a large blanket. 'You too, Mother — you look just as bedraggled as the girl. Best get to your room, we'll sort things out here. Sister Flora will go with you. . . .'

'No — I'll manage. I'm just grateful to be home. Stay with the child — I'll be down again in a little while — and Sister Clare, a mug of hot milk for the girl would be a good idea and some of your nice hot tea would be very welcome.'

Slipping off her shoes and raincoat she left them in a heap in the hall and went upstairs to her room, stripped off all her wet clothes, put on her nightie and warm dressing gown, then towelled her hair dry and ran a comb through it.

The hall was empty when she came downstairs again so she hurried to the kitchen guessing that's where they would be. She was right. The girl, clutching the blanket around her, was sitting at the table, one hand holding a large china mug. Her cheeks were still pale and she was obviously tired to death. Her clothes were in a heap by the washing machine and Joan's own grey raincoat, with the crumpled veil beside it, were hanging on the pulley at ceiling height and her black leather shoes were upside down on the rack above the Rayburn. Strangely, the girl still had on the one strappy sandal. It looked absurd peeping out from underneath the blanket.

'Where are you from?'

'How did you get here?'

'Are you alone?'

'She won't give up the sandal, Mother. She put it back on again after we wrapped her up warm, but she hasn't asked for the other.'

They were all trying to speak at once. The tired eyes of the girl looked confused, she shivered and said nothing.

'She won't say a jolly thing,' said Sister Imelda. 'Maybe she's foreign.'

'Sure, she hasn't had even a sip of that nice hot milk yet. She just sits there all quiet. It frightens me.' Sister Clare poured a mug of tea for her superior.

'A little quiet would be a good thing for us all, I think.' Joan sat beside the girl and told them about the car she'd found and her journey home in the rain and the discovery of their guest. She didn't mention the failing of the MOT. Somehow it seemed of little importance compared with their immediate problem.

'She isn't foreign.' She smiled at the girl. 'You understood me, didn't you? Out there in the rain?'

'Yes.'

The nuns sighed in unison.

'Drink your milk, child, then you must have a warm bath before we tuck you up in bed.' Joan sipped her tea and the girl, with her gaze fixed on Joan, began to drink the milk.

The kitchen was quiet now except for the ticking of the clock.

Suddenly, the girl, still looking at Joan, said, 'You lot — who are you? Nuns or something?'

'Yes, child — this is the Stella Maris Convent. It's the only house at the end of this lane. Did you intend to come here?'

'No.'

'Where were you heading? You must have taken a wrong turn.'

The girl drank deeply. The nuns seemed not to be breathing as they waited for her to reply as if the slightest sound would result in the girl's silence again.

'I was running out of gas — turned off the main road — didn't want to be on the main road.'

'Not very wise, dear, you could have got quite lost. This is a very bleak area — no houses for miles. If you'd taken a turning further on you could have broken down and not been found for hours — maybe even a day,' Joan said gently.

There was silence again before the girl said, 'Forever would have been better — don't ever want to be found. . . .' Suddenly she closed her eyes and almost toppled off the chair.

Sister Emma grabbed the mug as Joan put out an arm to steady the girl.

'No bath tonight, I think!' she said firmly. 'We must get her into bed as soon as possible. Goodness only knows how long she's been driving to be as exhausted as this.'

'What she just said, Mother.' Sister Clare put her hand on Joan's arm and spoke softly. 'She sounds — in despair.'

'A good sleep, that's what she needs,' Joan said quietly. 'We can talk in the morning. She's desperately tired — doesn't know what she's saying.'

Joan got up and helped the girl to her feet, wrapping the blanket more warmly around her, but what the girl had said disturbed her deeply.

'A hot water bottle would be a good thing — jolly comforting is a hot water bottle.' Sister Imelda took the big kettle off the stove, went over to the sink and filled it.

'Won't take long to heat up,' she said, placing it back on the hot-plate.

'Good thinking, Sister — and she can have my clean nightie. It's in the airing cupboard, second shelf.' Joan felt a little dizzy. Bed would be a very welcome place tonight.

Sister Imelda unscrewed the stopper on the hot water bottle. 'Do you know what?' she said, 'I do believe we've got ourselves a "wanderer" at last.'

The guest room seemed cosy and welcoming. Clare had gone on ahead and had plugged in the little one-bar electric heater and already the room was warming up. Joan had almost forgotton how tiny it was, but it felt secure and safe. In the morning the window would reveal the back garden with the meadow behind it and the seashore beyond. In the summer when the window was open, the sea could be heard, the waves rushing across the shingle like a sound of distant applause. The walls were plain white with no ornament. A crucifix above the bed, a chair and a small chest of drawers on top of which was a plain little vase placed on a doily crocheted by sister Clare, so that a guest could have a flower to lift the spirits, and beside that, a small plaster statue of the Virgin.

The girl's hair had dried and lay in blonde waves across the pillow. Her face was still pale; she probably needed a good nourishing meal, but not now. Sister Joan could see that she was too tired. Her young body needed rest now above anything else. She realized that she hadn't eaten anything herself since lunchtime and it was now nearly seven o'clock. It seemed like midnight. As the other sisters left the room Joan stayed a moment longer to see if the girl would ask for anything, or tell her something quietly and alone. As she looked down at her the girl's eyes opened.

'Thank you,' she said.

'It is our privilege child, to give what help and shelter we can to all those in need.'

'Don't be daft! How often do you drag people like me off the road?'

Joan had to grin. 'Never have, actually.'

'Then if I'm the first, it probably is a privilege.'

Cheeky little minx! thought Joan, but she didn't say so.

'You the head one here?' The girl looked at her quizzically.

'Yes, I'm the Mother Superior.'

'Can I stay — for a while?'

'Well — yes, of course you can.' Joan sat down on the end of the bed, her legs weak with fatigue. 'But you haven't told us your name yet — we have to know who you are. You do have a name, don't you?'

The girl didn't answer the question. She said, 'My car. . . .'

'Yes, child.'

'Get it here — please get it inside somewhere! You must have a garage or something?'

'Sister Imelda will fetch it in the morning,' Joan assured her. 'Don't worry about it, nobody's going to steal it. It's too ghastly a night — even for thieves.'

'Now, get it now!' The girl raised herself on one elbow. 'It must be out of sight. I don't want anyone to know I'm here.' She began to cry. 'My other sandal — don't leave it out there, find it — you must find it!'

Joan patted the hand that was clutching the bedspread. 'Hush now — it's OK, nobody's going to hurt you. You're safe here.' Her mind whirled — what was this all about? What was the child running from? Quite obviously, she was trying to get away from something or someone.

'Get the car, please get the car! The keys are still in it. Tell that big nun to go and get it now!' Her face was contorted with effort, weariness and anger.

'I'll do my best, but poor Sister Imelda, how can I send her out on a night like this?'

'She'll have to do it if you tell her to!'

Joan supressed a harsh reply; after all this was a wanderer. Maybe not an ideal one but a wanderer just the same and she was bound by her vows to do her best for the child. Sister Imelda wouldn't say no. She would be only too keen to get her hands on the car, whatever the weather. She could syphon some petrol from Sister Ford then take the old car the one mile up the lane, leave it on the verge and come back in the girl's car. It somehow didn't seem so difficult after all and she hadn't exactly promised Len Harvey that the car wouldn't be taken out again. It was just the sort of challenge that Sister Imelda would enjoy — it shouldn't take too long. The rain was bound to stop soon and then, tomorrow, she could walk up the lane and collect Sister Ford.

'I'll see what I can do,' she said.

The girl relaxed into the pillow and sighed, her eyes drooping with exhaustion.

'Thanks,' she whispered.

Joan stood up. 'Now, in return I would like you to tell me your name,' she said.

The girl glanced at the small plaster statue on the chest of drawers and then at Joan.

'It's — Mary.' She shivered a little. 'Mary

Winter.'

Sister Joan walked over to the door, opened it and, turning, said, 'Goodnight then — Mary Winter.' She went through onto the landing and closed the door of the little guest room quietly behind her.

The nuns were all in the kitchen and had made more tea and a light meal. They were totally put out of their routine by the happenings of the day. So was Joan.

'Imelda, I have an awfully big favour to ask of you —' she began.

'If you want me to go and get the girl's car, I'd be delighted to do it,' the portly nun grinned.

'Well, yes, if you really don't mind. She left the keys in it. . . .'

Sister Imelda downed the last dregs of her tea, put the mug on the table and rubbed her hands together. 'What an exciting day this has turned out to be — I'll syphon some petrol out of Sister Ford. I'll be back in a brace of shakes!' She went out of the kitchen as if the wind was at her back.

'What would we do without Imelda?' Sister Clare gathered up the mugs and put them in the sink.

'I don't know, Clare — I really don't

know.' Joan laughed for the first time that day.

They heard Sister Ford going up the drive; the sound of her engine faded away and left only the drumming of the rain. Joan felt worried now. Maybe she should have been firmer with the girl and not put one of her nuns in a potentially dangerous situation. As she hadn't mentioned the MOT Sister Imelda probably thought everything was OK despite the fact that she must have known about the bald tyre. She always had faith that something or someone would turn up to help. After all, she would probably think that as Len Harvey had dozens of tyres out at the back of the garage, surely he would have spared one for Sister Ford. He'd probably fixed it this afternoon and the MOT was in the bag. The rain beat against the kitchen window and Joan waited anxiously.

They heard the approach of the other car — a different sound entirely from the older one. It went past the house and on into the barn. They heard the big doors slam shut, then in a little while the front door opened and closed again.

Sister Imelda came into the kitchen, rosy cheeked and wet through, carrying the hold-all that had been in the girl's car and tread-

40

ing mud on Sister Clare's pristine floor.

'I've got it!' she cried. 'I've put it in the barn and — you'll never guess — it's a *Porsche!*' She put the bag down on the table. 'And what's more — it's a *red* one! I knew we'd get a jolly miracle!' She took off her anorak.

'Sister Imelda, it doesn't belong to us.' Joan took the purple anorak and put it over the back of a chair beside the Rayburn.

'But — we could borrow it — just for a little while. I'll drive. Now Monday won't be a problem. We can take Sister Flora to the dentist, no worries!'

'What makes you think we won't be going in our own car?' Joan gave her a quizzical look.

Imelda smiled. 'I'm not as green as I'm cabbage-looking you know!' she laughed. 'We'd have needed a miracle to get her through this time. I thought the miracle might have been Len Harvey — but on second thoughts, he's much too honest. Tell us now, did the old girl pass?'

Joan shook her head. 'Not this time — or ever, I'm afraid.'

Old Sister Flora clasped her hands together. 'Oh, Mother — and I made a banner too!'

Sister Imelda grinned. 'But now we have

the Porsche! Surely that's a miracle?'

'It's still not ours — but maybe for Monday, if Mary doesn't mind.'

'So — it's Mary is it. Sure, she wouldn't tell us her name. Mary — that's nice.' Sister Clare smiled. 'Mary — Mary what?'

'She said, Mary Winter.' As she spoke Joan thought how apt, how just too coincidental. She remembered the girl glancing at the statue on the chest of drawers and the shiver she gave as she settled down into the warm bed. She imagined her lying upstairs in the guest room, sleeping like a baby. I don't know where you've come from, or why you're running away, she thought, but I get the feeling that your name is certainly not Mary Winter.

CHAPTER FOUR

Sister Joan woke just before it was time to get up. She lay and waited for Sister Clare to ring the large brass hand-bell and call 'Good morning, God bless you' as she walked past each room. It was traditional to ring the bell and Sister Clare stuck to tradition wherever she could, despite the fact that she had a digital alarm clock to wake her in time to ring it. It was a surprise when, instead of the expected clanging, there was a gentle knock on her door.

'Good morning, God bless you.' Sister Clare opened the door slightly, popped her head around it and put on the light. 'Didn't want to ring the bell this morning for fear of disturbing the child — bit early for her, don't you think?'

'Very thoughtful of you, Sister. We'll let her sleep on as long as she wants. No doubt she'll be hungry by breakfast.'

Sister Clare smiled. 'She'll eat us out of

house and home, no doubt. Young people are always hungry. I'll wake the others.' She slipped out of sight and closed the door quietly.

Sister Joan yawned and stretched. It was still dark but she was accustomed to rising early, they all were. She got out of bed, washed and put on the fresh habit and veil that replaced those hanging downstairs on the pulley over the Rayburn in the kitchen. Her shoes were dry, clean and had been put just inside her door, probably while she was asleep — dear Sister Clare. Putting on her veil reminded her of the events of the evening before and the finding of the young girl lying in the muddy lane. She was eager to talk to her again, quietly and alone. There was a mystery about her, a fact which must be obvious to the other nuns although she doubted that they had the same feeling about Mary Winter not being the girl's real name. However, now was not the time to think about anything but chapel and morning prayers. She took a sip of water from the glass by her bed. How she longed for a cup of tea, but prayers came first.

Going out onto the landing, she closed the bedroom door and waited for the other nuns to join her. Together they filed quietly down the stairs and across the hall to the little chapel. It was dark inside except for the one small electric lamp illuminating the altar, Sister Joan switched on the main light and they all took their usual places. This was their first duty of the day.

'I'm positively dying for a cup of tea!' Sister Imelda rubbed her hands together as the sisters gathered in the cosy kitchen.

'It'll be ready soon.' Sister Clare put the big kettle on the hotplate.

They all sat around the kitchen table. It was a time that Sister Joan enjoyed. They chattered like magpies about the happenings of the night before and of the chores they had to do that day. Who could be spared to help whom and if the oldest brown hen had really stopped laying. There was a refectory and Sister Joan insisted that they all gathered there for the evening meal, but the kitchen was used for breakfast and lunch because they were not always together at those times. It all depended on what the duties of the day demanded. Sometimes one or other of them would be with a member of the parish all night if she was needed. Some sisters, after that first welcome cup of tea, would grab a slice of toast and hurry off to the garden or to collect the eggs and see to the chickens. Sister Joan knew that

Clare was always at the ready with a sandwich or a bowl of soup. If Sister Imelda was head and shoulders in someone's lawnmower repair, she would take out a snack to the barn and remind her that she should have a break. Sister Joan could always depend on Clare. She knew she had to tell them about the letter from the Mother House soon, they had a right to know, but they looked so happy and excited about the new turn their lives had taken with the arrival of their wanderer, that she didn't have the heart for it — not today.

Sister Clare poured the tea. 'Now, is everyone here for breakfast this morning — nobody waltzing off to jobs that can't wait?'

Everyone said, 'Yes, I'm here.'

'Good. It's porridge today — these mornings are geting cold enough for it — and toast if you're wanting it.' She bustled about her kitchen like a mother hen.

Sister Joan smiled. 'I don't know how you do it, Clare, looking after all of us so well. It must be hard work.'

'We're only eight, Mother. Now if we were five thousand I'd have something to worry about.' She laughed and stirred the pot.

There was a lull in the conversation and Sister Joan sensed that they were all wanting to ask the same thing.

'I've left the child to sleep for a little longer,' she said. 'We'll wait until she decides to make an appearance. It shouldn't be too long; she must be terribly hungry.'

'Should I take her up some breakfast on a tray?'

'I don't think so, Sister, unless it gets very late. Then I think we should check up on her. Maybe take a cup of tea. I can't imagine her lying in bed for very long. I think she has a lot on her mind.'

'Do you know where she's come from? Did she say anything to you last night?' Sister Flora took a sip of tea. 'She seems to be running away from something; she was very distressed.'

'She was all het up about her car and I'm not surprised: it's very new and very expensive. How did a young girl like that come by such a vehicle?' Sister Imelda leaned her elbows on the table and rested her chin in her hands. 'It's a dream to drive. Just imagine Len Harvey's face if he saw us buzzing around in that!'

'*Elbows!* Imelda,' said Sister Clare. 'Here's your porridge, you can have more if you need it.'

'The child didn't say much last night,' said Sister Joan. 'She was concerned about the car — quite rude to me in fact — and also

47

about the missing sandal. It definitely seems as if she wants to hide. No doubt she'll tell us more, she was very tired. She'll be a different person today, you can be sure of that.'

'Maybe she's running from the Mafia.' Sister Emma's eyes were round and bright with excitement.

'Or the police?'

'Or a gang of crooks?'

'She could be a jewel thief who's stolen a valuable diamond from someone terribly rich and famous. . . .'

'She's probably stolen the car — and now it's in *our* barn.' Suddenly, they all had something to say.

'Sisters, your imaginations are running away with you.' Sister Joan held up her hand. 'The poor girl has a problem that just needs a few days to sort out. Some young people are very impulsive. She'll work it all out soon and then she'll be off. If we can help her we will do our best, but we must wait and not jump to conclusions. We must assume that the car is certainly her own — we mustn't weave stories.'

Sister Clare indicated a chair in the corner of the kitchen. 'Her holdall is still there — maybe if we had a quick look. . . .'

'No, Sister, certainly not. We shouldn't pry into someone's private things; it wouldn't be right.' Sister Joan felt slightly guilty because — having already noticed the bag was there — she was longing to do just that. We must wait for the child, be patient and she will confide in us — I'm sure of that. I shall take the holdall upstairs and put it outside her door. It was remiss of me not to take it to her room last night. Now, Sisters, — grace.' They bowed their heads while she said the prayer. She smiled as they ate quietly. Sister Clare's porridge was the best.

'My goodness, Clare, this is very good!' Sister Imelda smiled. 'May I have a little more? I've given Mrs Robinson's lawn-mower a complete medical but I still have to sharpen the blades, so I'm going to need the energy. I promised her Saturday after-noon — she's bound to be here directly after lunch!'

As they all filed out after breakfast, Sister Joan thought of the girl lying upstairs, maybe awake now, nervous in a strange room and bed, not knowing what to do. 'I think I'll take a cup of tea to the child,' she said.

'Good idea.' Sister Clare took a cup and saucer from the dresser and putting them on the table she picked up a large enamel teapot from the Rayburn and poured a cup.

'Poor little soul — she'll feel so lost if she's lying up there awake.'

Half way up the stairs with the tea, Sister Joan remembered that she hadn't brought the holdall. Never mind, she thought, plenty of time. At the top of the stairs she paused. Am I imagining it, she thought? She strained her ears — yes, the sound was coming from the guest room. She moved closer to the door. The girl was sobbing, crying quietly with long shuddering breaths as if her very soul was weeping.

Sister Joan knocked briefly and opened the door, her heart aching at the sound of such distress. The morning light filtered through the curtains and lit the girl's face on the pillow. Her cheeks were wet with tears and she turned her head from side to side as if in great trouble. Sister Joan moved quietly into the room and put the tea on the little side table. Maybe the child had taken ill in the night. How careless not to have checked up on her earlier.

'Mary, whatever is the matter?' Reaching out to touch the girl's forehead she said, 'You feel so hot. . . .' She paused and looked closer. Mary was still sleeping. 'Oh, my dear,' she whispered. The girl hadn't heard her come into the room, nor had she heard Sister Joan speak to her or felt the soft touch on her forehead.

Mary's lips moved, 'Please — please don't leave me . . . not now . . . not now!' She drew a deep breath and more tears ran down her face and onto the pillow. 'I can't be alone . . . please help. . . .' Then at last she breathed more regularly and evenly as if at least one part of the nightmare was over.

Sister Joan longed to smooth back the hair that stuck damply to the girl's face, to hold her close and tell her that she was safe. Instead, she turned and went back onto the landing, closing the door quietly behind her. They would surely know soon enough what Mary's problem was. But for the present, Sister Joan decided it would be wiser to leave her to the privacy of her dreams.

CHAPTER FIVE

'If we save the brussels sprouts for tomorrow and have the cabbage tonight with the macaroni cheese, that'll work quite well.' Sister Clare discussed the week's menus with Sister Joan, as was their Saturday morning task after breakfast.

'That sounds excellent Clare. I don't know why I should go over the menus with you — you always turn out such good meals, it seems hardly worth while.'

'Ah, but Mother — it's traditional. We've always discussed the food together and I — well, I sort of like it.'

'So do I Clare, so do I.'

'I didn't know what to do — or where I should go.'

A voice from behind made them both jump. Sister Joan got up from her chair quickly and turned to see the girl standing in the doorway, her blonde hair tangled around her face. She was clutching the bedspread from the guest room around her shoulders, the hem of the nightgown just above her bare feet. Her face was now devoid of the outrageous make-up she had been wearing the night before. Her eyes were violet blue and fringed with long lashes but the dark circles of weeping were around them. Her skin was perfect and her lips rosy with sleep. Only her fingernails, long and coloured bright pink, spoiled the illusion of a Botticelli angel. She lifted her free hand and brushed back her long blonde hair over one ear, revealing four gold ear studs in a line from lobe to tip. The celestial image was shattered completely.

'Oh, my! I didn't give her a dressing gown!' Sister Clare moved forward, beckoning the girl toward her. 'Come right in, my dear. I'll be back in a jiffy. There's a spare one in the airing cupboard.' She hurried through the door.

'You must be starving,' said Sister Joan. 'Sit down child, we'll get you something to eat.'

'Someone brought me tea, thanks. I'm still very thirsty.' The girl looked around her nervously as if ready to take flight at any moment.

'Another nice cup of tea then?'

The girl nodded. 'Yes, thanks, or orange juice?'

'I'm afraid we've no juice, dear — coffee, if you like?'

Mary hesitated as if any decision was difficult for her. 'Tea will be nice.'

Sister Clare returned from the airing cupboard with a large dressing gown. She handed it to the girl who put it on, shedding the bedspread onto the kitchen floor.

'It's very big,' Mary said. The sleeves of the gown hung down beyond her painted fingernails.

'It's nice and warm — that's all that matters at the moment, dear.' Sister Clare settled the collar around the girl's neck, fastened the top button and turned up the cuffs.

'Can I sit down?'

'Of course, child.' Sister Joan pulled a chair from where it had been tucked under the table.

Mary looked around the room nervously before she sat down. 'Is there anyone else here?'

Sister Joan smiled. 'Just Clare and me, sorting out the menus for the week. The others are at their various jobs around the place.'

Mary was silent for a while, then she suddenly straightened in her chair and placed her clenched fist on the table. 'Did you get my car?'

'Yes — Sister Imelda put it in the barn with ours.'

'No one's come here looking for me, have they?'

Sister Joan drew her own chair closer to the girl and sat down beside her. 'Child, there's no need to be afraid. No one has been here. This is a convent. We ask you no questions. (Oh, how she longed to ask Mary so many questions.) We're here to take in anyone who needs shelter. We've given you a bed for the night and have taken care of you. If you wish to share a problem we're here to listen.' She smiled. 'Now, Clare will give you a nice cup of tea and you'll feel all the better for it.'

Tears welled up in Mary's eyes. 'I-I want to stay if I can. I can't leave today. I'm so tired — I feel so sick. I've got some money, I can pay you. Please let me stay!'

'Of course you may stay, just as long as you feel the need,' Sister Joan reassured her.

Sister Clare took a cup and saucer from the dresser and poured tea. 'You're sick from lack of nourishment, that's what! I'll get you breakfast right away. Now, here's tea; drink it up before you dehydrate!'

Sister Joan noticed that Mary's hand shook as she picked up the cup and drank. As Sister Clare clattered about with the preparations for one more breakfast, she waited and watched the colour begin to come into the girl's cheeks. Sister Joan thought how very thin she looked. Mary's hand shook again as she placed the cup back on the saucer.

'Is that better, child?' Sister Clare touched the girl's shoulder lightly.

Mary shrank from the touch as if she had been stung. 'You mustn't tell anyone I'm here — please don't tell!'

'For goodness' sake, child — and who would I be telling?' Clare was the kindest person and Sister Joan could see that she had been hurt by the girl's reaction.

'Mary, you have crossed our path and are under our roof and in our care. We would want to help you if you're in some sort of trouble.' Sister Joan was intrigued by this child who had come to them out of the storm. Their Rule declared that they were to give food, shelter and comfort — nothing else except, if they could, the means to help the traveller to continue a journey. Being inquisitive was certainly not in their remit. But how can I help it, she thought? Times have changed since our Order was formed so long ago. It was a hard world then but now there were new dangers and a young girl on her own — well, maybe it did give her the right to find out more about Mary.

To Sister Joan's surprise, Mary's eyes filled with tears that trickled down her cheeks unhindered until they dropped off her chin. Her lower lip trembled like a baby's and she dashed the tears away with the over-long cuff of the dressing gown. 'I'm still so tired!' she whispered.

'Didn't you sleep well? Was the bed not comfortable?' Sister Clare's voice was full of concern.

'Oh, yes — it was OK, but I didn't move all night and I ache so much now.' Mary rubbed the back of her neck.

'A good hot bath with a handful of salt in it will soon put that to rights.' Sister Joan noticed that Clare took the chance of putting an arm around the girl's shoulders. This time it wasn't shaken off, but there was no acceptance of the gesture. 'We should have given you more than a lick and a promise last night but you were so exhausted we thought the best thing was to get you right into bed.'

Mary looked at Sister Joan and said, 'I could have died out there in the rain, if you hadn't found me. You're being so kind to me and I'm such a bother. I'm a spoiled brat, you know — everyone says —'

'Who, Mary? Who would call you that?' Sister Joan took her hand. Mary flinched at her touch. The child is on the defensive, she thought like a small terrified creature.

Mary withdrew her hand slowly and said, 'I'm hungry.'

Sister Joan realized that now was not the time and that the girl wasn't ready to tell them anything yet. She could see that Clare could hardly contain her curiosity.

'What do you usually have for breakfast then?'

How clever of you Clare, thought Joan. The reply would indicate, maybe, the girl's status. Did she get her own breakfast or — using the expensive car and the long pink fingernails as a yardstick — did someone else do all that for her?

Mary looked up at Clare. 'Anything you have will do,' she said.

'Porridge?'

Mary blanched and put her hand over her mouth. Her face became quite grey again. 'I really don't feel very well.'

'That's because you're so starved. I'll do you some nice toast and maybe later you'll fancy something more substantial.' Sister Clare cut two thick slices of bread, placed them in the toasting cage and put them onto the hotplate of the Rayburn, closing the lid down on top. 'Nothing like hot buttered toast to put fresh heart into a girl,' she smiled.

Sister Joan got up from her chair. 'I really must go and do some work. I have a lot of letters to write and some phone calls to make. Sister will see that you have everything you need and, by the way, your hold-all is over there on the chair. I was going to take it up to your room, but I forgot all about it last night. Your trousers, top and underthings are all clean and drying on the pulley up there.' She pointed to the warm spot above the stove near the ceiling.

Mary looked up. 'Are they dry yet? It's all I've got to wear.'

'You've no suitcase with your holiday things then?' Sister Clare asked innocently.

'Just a change of undies — I was in a hurry. Did you — did you look in my bag?'

'Certainly not — we'd never do that. Your personal possessions are your own affair; we'd never dream of doing such a thing.' Sister Clare became quite pink with embarrasment.

Mary leaned forward slightly. 'There's private things in my bag.' Then a look of relief came over her pale face. 'You're ever so honest. I'm so glad you found me. You'll hide me, won't you? Please — I don't want to run any further.'

'Who are you running from? Can't you tell us what's troubling you? Maybe we can help.' Joan took her hand. Mary didn't withdraw it.

Her eyes met Joan's and held her gaze. 'I-I can't tell you, not yet. I'm not ready to. I haven't done anything really terrible. It's just that — Oh, please don't ask me — not now!'

Sister Joan put her forefinger against the girl's lips. 'Hush, child, whatever your problem is — please know that we are your friends.' The small white hand trembled like a little bird, but it remained in Joan's and after a while returned the pressure ever so slightly. Joan felt warmth and trust pass between them only fleetingly — but it was there.

There were only a few of them in the kitchen for lunch. Sister Joan sat at the head of the table with Sisters Clare, Flora, Imelda, Emma and Mary Winter. Mary's clothes were still hanging damply above them on the pulley, so she was looking rather strange in a white blouse, grey cardigan and skirt. A large pleat had been taken in the skirt at the waist with a safety pin. They'd found a pair of shoes that nearly fitted and some thick long woollen socks. She seemed to be feeling much better and had done her hair in an outrageous style with something that looked rather like a large plastic bulldog clip — bright red. Perhaps, Sister Joan thought, she's wearing it as a small rebellion against having to be clothed in the cast-off habit of one of their nuns, who had grown in size and vocation and had been moved to pastures new.

'Is this all of you?' Mary glanced around the table.

'No, dear — Sisters Louise and Amy are rotovating a piece of garden just beyond the orchard — they've taken their lunch with them — and Sister Madeline is away visiting her family. There are eight of us in all.'

'I thought there would be dozens of you all over the place.'

'No, we're a very small community.'

When Sister Clare had served the soup, and the bread had been cut into slices and placed on a large dish in the centre of the table, Sister Joan clasped her hands and just as Mary dipped her spoon into her soup, she began to say grace. Mary left the spoon in the bowl and bowed her head. So, thought Joan, you're not accustomed to this

61

in your household. After grace, she went on, 'Thank you, Mary, for bearing with us. It's an old-fashioned thing to do but we still say grace here.'

'We always did at home,' Mary said, her cheeks flushing, 'but if you're living most of the time in and out of hotels, well, you forget.'

Another piece of the jigsaw, thought Sister Joan. She glanced over at Sister Clare who raised one eyebrow but said nothing.

'Have a lot of holidays then, do you?' Sister Imelda broke a piece of bread off her slice and put it in her soup. 'Been to lots of exciting places? Up mountains, down rivers, Taj Mahal and all that? I'd always planned to do the world in a Land Rover but the vocation took over and that was that.' She smiled, dipped her spoon in the soup and sipped with a delicacy that belied her appearance. 'Where were you off to yesterday then, before you ran out of petrol?'

There was a silence around the table. Mary kept her eyes on the soup and said nothing. There was a feeling that everyone was waiting. Sister Joan frowned at Imelda and gave an almost imperceptible shake of her head. Too many questions, her eyes said.

'Sorry,' Sister Imelda said quietly. 'I talk too much; bit rude to do that at table.

Wonderful drop of soup, Sister.'

Sister Clare smiled and there was another long silence.

'Are those all the clothes you have?' Sister Emma gazed up at the pulley.

Mary said, 'Yes.'

'What are the little red things with the black lace on?'

'That's enough, Sister,' said Clare. 'They're her — her scanties.'

Emma looked puzzled.

'Her underclothes,' said Sister Joan gently.

'Oh!' Emma's eyes widened.

'I know what you're thinking.' Sister Clare took a deep breath. 'Wouldn't keep a sparrow warm, so they wouldn't — considering the time of year. Did you not bring a warm coat with you, dear?' she said to Mary.

Mary shook her head but said nothing.

Sister Flora put a piece of bread carefully into her mouth. 'My tooth is getting more and more wobbly you know.'

Mary began to giggle. Sister Joan imagined it was because of the sheer stress of her situation.

'Oh! I'm so sorry but — but that sounded so funny.' She briefly put her napkin against her mouth. 'What's wrong with your tooth?' she turned to Sister Flora who was sitting next to her.

'There was an abcess on it so I think it died,' she said. 'I'm going to the dentist on Monday. I expect he'll take it out.'

Mary's face softened. 'Oh, you poor thing, that's awful. Isn't there anything that can be done to save it?'

'No, it isn't worth it. The dentist said it would be better out, so it's best just to forget it.' Sister Flora's gentle face broke into a smile. 'You musn't worry, dear.'

Sister Joan noted Mary's look of sympathy and compassion. So, there was kindness in the child.

Suddenly, Mary said, 'I think you're very brave — I hate the dentist — I had to have a brace for ages. It nearly ruined my self-confidence!'

Sister Joan smiled. 'My dear, a lost tooth means nothing at all to us, provided it doesn't interfere with eating and drinking and the digestion. Getting Sister Flora to the dentist in town is the main problem.'

'But you've got a car — you brought me here in it.'

Sister Joan sighed. 'I was on my way back from a failed MOT when I found you, Mary. We have, in fact, no car at all I'm afraid.'

'Can't you get another one?'

'Another car is quite out of the question

at the moment, dear.'

'There's mine — you can use mine. Will you let me stay until Monday?' Mary leaned forward eagerly.

Sister Joan looked into her eyes. 'But you wanted us to hide it yesterday — remember? It was important to you for the car not to be seen.'

Mary looked at Sister Flora who was glancing from one to the other of them as if she was at a tennis match. 'Please take my car, it's — I'm far enough away — no one is going to connect it with me.'

Sister Joan put down her spoon and clasped her hands together on the table top. 'Mary, can't you tell us what's going on? This has all gone too far now. You've said so much — you have to tell us what it is you're running from, because running you certainly seem to be. We're your friends — talk to us, child!'

In an instant, Mary's face changed from calm to panic. 'I'm not a crook or anything, please believe that — I can't tell you anything yet — I really can't. I haven't done anything bad — honest I haven't! I just have to have some space. Get away, think, just for a while.'

'Then all I can say is — thank you, Mary. We'd be very grateful for the loan of the car and of course we will abide by your wishes. You may have all the peace and quiet you need here with us,' said Sister Joan. She was worried now that she had gone too far — frightened the girl too much and that she would run again, giving them no chance at all of helping her.

'I'd like to stay longer than just to Monday. I'll pay, I've got some money. It wouldn't be an insult or anything, if I gave you some money?' Her eyes were wide with hope.

'Oh, Mary.' Sister Joan thought of the couple in the Range Rover who had wanted to pay for bed and breakfast accommodation and whom she had refused. It seemed that it was time for things to change after all. 'You will be very welcome to stay for as long as you need. Provided you can accept us just as we are.'

Mary smiled again. 'I'll be as quiet as a mouse, promise' — she closed her eyes — 'cross my heart and hope to die!' She made a cross over her heart like a schoolchild, took up her spoon and dipped it into her soup.

'Are the Mafia after you?' Sister Emma whispered, wide-eyed. 'If they are we'll hide you. They'll never find you here!'

'Emma, don't be so dramatic. Of course

the Mafia aren't after Mary — are they?'
Sister Imelda's spoon was poised above her
soup bowl.

'No — no, of course not.' Mary looked
confused. 'I just want to be on my own for
a while. I can't tell you — not yet. My
head's not sorted.'

There was a silence, then Sister Imelda
said, 'If we can borrow the car on Monday
then, can I drive it?'

'Yes, of course you can,' said Mary.

'Jolly dee!' said Imelda quietly, and continued to eat her lunch. 'Tuck in, everyone,
before it gets cold.' She turned to Mary.
'Insurance OK and all that?'

'Yes, of course! But Sister.' Her voice was
nervous again. 'You'll need petrol — I'll give
you a bit of money for that and — please
park it somewhere sort of quiet, won't you?'

Imelda frowned. 'Not pinched, is it?'

'No! Of course not. I just don't want, you
know, any connection with me. Number
plate, and all that.'

Imelda smiled. 'Quiet as snow at midnight
outside Mr Macpherson's surgery. No worries about anyone even knowing we're
there.'

Sister Joan groaned inwardly at the
thought of three of them — for she was
determined to accompany Imelda and Flora

67

on Monday — driving around in a bright red Porsche having failed an MOT in their own old car the Friday before and their financial position not entirely unknown at least to Len Harvey and his lad. She couldn't share Imelda's confidence about them not being noticed. Dear Lord, she thought, what is our vocation getting us into? She almost suggested they abandon the idea entirely and beg a lift from Bill Murray up at the farm, but somehow the die seemed to be cast. The appointment was for late afternoon — it would be dark, the girl had been so kind, she was gaining confidence in them. Imelda's cheeks were glowing — oh, dear Lord — let it be OK.

'It looks as though Monday's appointment with the dentist will prove to be a little more exciting than we ever imagined,' Sister Clare said quietly, as she ladled a little more soup into Mary's bowl.

CHAPTER SIX

'You can come to chapel with us if you want to. Father Anderson always comes to say mass for us on Sundays.' Sister Joan helped Mary to tuck in the bedclothes neatly as she helped her tidy her room. The girl seemed to have no idea how to do the simplest domestic chore.

'No, thanks. The priest doesn't know I'm here, does he?' Mary was on the defensive again.

'Not yet dear, but he's bound to ask how we are and if there's any news since last Sunday. There very seldom is, but I have something I want to consult him about afterwards.' She would confide in Father Anderson about the letter from the Mother House. Maybe he would be able to supply an answer to their problem, but she doubted it.

'Is it about me? Are you going to talk about me?'

'No, Mary — something else entirely.'

'You're going to tell him about me, though, aren't you?'

'I shall tell him that we have a visitor for a few days.'

'He'll want to see me, won't he?'

'No, dear, of course not, you're our guest. He'd have no reason to want to see you. Unless, of course, you want to see him?' Joan could hear the panic in Mary's voice.

'No, — no I don't.'

Sister Joan turned down the sheet neatly and arranged the pillow. 'Then you don't have to see Father at all, dear.'

'I just don't want to see — anybody. Has anyone found my other sandal yet? I have to have it. It must be lying out there somewhere.'

'Everything will be fine, Mary, just take your time and relax. One of us will find the sandal, don't worry. It's a bright morning. Why don't you wrap up warm and take a walk down on the beach. It'll do you good.'

'Beach?'

'Yes, just take the little path down beside the garden and past the orchard. It leads directly onto the shore and it's quite private, you won't meet a soul. You can hear the sea if you open the window.'

Mary lifted the latch and opened it to the

chilly air. 'Oh yes, I can hear it, I didn't know we were so near the sea. I can smell it too. It reminds me of buckets and spades and the old sunhat that Mum —' She stopped and closed the window again, turning to help Sister Joan smooth down the bedspread.

Sister Joan smiled. 'It's strange, the things that spark off memories. Scents, tunes, sounds, all sorts of things. What about your family, Mary? Your mother must be very worried by now. We have a telephone if you want to make a call. . . .'

'No — not now! I've got my mobile anyway. Can I borrow Imelda's anorak? I think I'll go outside for a while.' Mary didn't meet Joan's gaze; the girl was being evasive again.

'Imelda's coat will be huge on you. It'll cover you from top to toe — you'll certainly be warm enough.' Sister Joan laughed, but quietly mourned the passing of the moment that might have brought her closer to the girl. They finished tidying the room then went out onto the landing, closing the door behind them.

As Mary ran down the stairs, she called back. 'There'll be no one to see me anyway, you said so. So it doesn't matter if I look like a purple yeti!' She laughed and dis-

71

appeared from view.

Sister Joan came down from the landing at a more ladylike pace and went to the chapel to prepare it for Father Anderson. She imagined Mary on the shore, the wind blowing through her blonde hair. For every missing person, she thought, there is a sea of anxious people somewhere.

After mass Sister Joan asked for tea on a tray to be brought to her study and as Father Anderson settled his portly frame down in the armchair by her desk she said, 'Father, I have been in a turmoil of anxiety for the past few days.'

'My dear Reverend Mother, what's happened?'

She told him all about the letter she'd had from the Mother House and about their financial situation. 'If we can't become solvent in the next year the history of our Order in this old house, will be at an end.' She couldn't help the tears that she had been bottling up. 'I haven't had the courage to tell the others yet. They know we're hard up but they accept that willingly. They only have a vague idea of how far things have gone. The house is in a state of disrepair. Nothing that shows inside very much at the moment but the roof is bad. It's leaking so much we've had to put an old tin bath in the attic to catch the drips. The battens and beams look terribly rotten. It's major work and we've not enough money. It all looks so hopeless, and to cap it all, Sister Imelda says that the boiler's on the way out.'

Father Anderson got up from the armchair and came over to pat her shoulder kindly. 'These old places — they need such a lot of maintenance and it's so expensive nowadays. The wiring probably needs seeing to as well.'

'Oh, Father!'

'Now, now, my dear. We'll have that cup of tea that Sister Clare has provided. A lot of problems are solved over a nice cup of tea.'

But the problem was not solved, not there and then. As she bade Father Anderson goodbye at the front door she realized that she had only passed on the worry to him. Money was scarce in their poor parish. He seemed to think that it would make sense to 'call it a day', let the old place go, and carry on their vocations elsewhere. 'We will miss you all very much though,' he said. 'You have done such a lot of good here. A wonderful support in the parish. However, let me go and put on my thinking cap.'

Ten thousand thinking caps won't mend the roof, she thought, as his car went up the driveway and through the ever-open iron gates. We're still at square one after all. I'm going to have to tell the Sisters now.

As she stood there on the doorstep in the quiet of the winter morning, she wondered if Mary had found the little beach and the bay that they thought of as their own. The land ran down to the shore and no one had access to it but the nuns. Mary would have all the peace she needed down there. Sister Joan walked down the steps from the front door and around the corner of the house, from where she could see across the back garden to the little path that led down to the sea. There was no sign of Mary — then she heard a little cough.

'Has he gone?' Mary peeped out from behind the old oak tree in the middle of the lawn, the hood of the purple anorak pulled tight around her face, the fur around the brim making her look like a tiny mouse.

'Why, Mary! Didn't you fancy the beach after all?'

'It's a bit far from the house — might be someone down there.'

Sister Joan smiled and held out her hand. So — such was the girl's fear that she could only go as far as the old oak. What was this mystery? Oh, Mary! she thought as the girl came across the grass and clasped her offered hand, how long will you keep us waiting? Suddenly her own troubles seemed to have little importance in comparison to the secret fears of this girl. Her heart ached as she felt the thin fingers clasp her hand tight. Whatever problems of their own they had to bear, Mary must come first.

They walked together into the old house towards the warmth of the kitchen. Mary threw back the hood of her coat revealing the red bulldog clip that held her hair in place. The coat reached beyond her knees and she'd turned the sleeves back. She took it off and hung it on the hook by the door where no doubt Sister Imelda would put it on in haste, wondering why the sleeves had shrunk. 'You were right about that old coat being warm,' she smiled.

The nuns were drinking tea and listening to the one small portable radio that accompanied them from kitchen to sewing-room and to anywhere they were gathered together in recreation. They were listening to the news.

'Oh, those poor, poor souls. Flooded out of their homes at this time of year.'

'The refugees — no roof over their heads and all that violence — we're so fortunate, Reverend Mother, we really are. If only we could do something.'

'We can pray.'

'Good hot soup — that's what!' Sister Clare seemed angry that she couldn't feed the third world as well as her own Sisters. 'Mary, dear girl, you look so pale. Sit down now — here's a nice mug of tea. Put your hands around it and they'll soon warm up.'

The radio crackled: '. . . the police are making a house-to-house enquiry about the girl who has been missing since Friday morning. There has been no sighting of either her or her boyfriend who was reported missing on the same day. Anyone wishing to give any information, please phone —' The announcer was cut short. Suddenly, Mary rose from her chair and with one sweeping movement she cleared the table of mugs, plates — and the radio, which smashed onto the terracotta tiles of the floor in hundreds of tiny pieces. She paused for a moment, wild-eyed, and then turning, ran through the doorway and up the stairs to her room. Sister Joan heard the door slam. Apart from the hissing of the kettle on the Rayburn, the kitchen and the Sisters were stunned to silence. The floor was wet with tea and crunchy with pottery and radio parts.

'What in heaven's name has possessed the child? That sort of thing's just not on you know —' Sister Imelda made an attempt to gather the radio parts together again. 'That little wireless is all we've got since the old black-and-white telly went on the blink!'

Sister Joan put a hand on her shoulder. 'Don't Imelda — it's hopeless, you'll never get it back together again.'

'It's our one and only jolly little radio and that wicked girl — what's got into her . . . ?'

Sister Flora began to cry and Emma put her arm around her. 'Oh Mother,' she said. 'What are we to do — not about the radio — but Mary? What's happening?'

Joan sat down at the table and indicated that her Sisters should do the same. 'I only know that the mystery of Mary grows deeper. That announcement on the radio disturbed her so much that she was reduced to an act of violence to silence it. Did anyone hear what it was all about?'

'I was worrying about the refugees,' said Sister Clare.

'I was only listening with half an ear,' sobbed Flora. 'My tooth, you see, it was aching.'

'We must be very careful now.' Sister Joan looked around at them all. 'She's very likely to run at this point. If we want to help her at all we must be compassionate and forgiving. Her problem is maybe much more than a family quarrel or minor tiff. I heard part of the announcement — about a boyfriend as well as a missing girl. We may have the missing girl — but, where is the boyfriend?'

'We've got to play it cool Sister.' Imelda's face was white and serious. 'Let her know we're still here to help.'

'We'll just go on as if nothing has happened — then maybe she'll spill the beans!' Sister Emma's face was flushed with excitement.

'Go on as if nothing's happened? I'll give her a good talking to, that's what, look at this mess all over my floor,' Sister Clare grumbled.

'We'll all give you a hand, Clare — while we think what to do.' Sister Joan got up from her chair and took up a broom from the corner of the kitchen. 'Best thing is to get back to normal as soon as possible.'

'Now that's where maybe I can help.' Imelda held the dustpan while Joan swept the pieces into it. 'Remember Christmas last year? My brother sent me a DIY crystal set — it's still in the box. I'll get it working in no time. Soon find the news and all that. See if it's got anything to do with our wanderer. No one mentioned the name Mary Winter in any of the reports that I heard. Maybe the girl just threw a paddy because she felt like it. You know — young people.'

Joan put a hand on her arm. 'There was no reason for a teenage tantrum — no reason at all. It must have had something to do with the announcement. I have a feeling that Mary may be the missing girl. Maybe I'm wrong but we must move very carefully. Whatever happens we must keep her here because goodness only knows where she'll go if she runs from us.'

'We'll have to be extra careful then,' said Sister Imelda, 'because we can't tie her up! She'll run if she wants to.'

Gradually the kitchen came to order and Sister Clare prepared lunch. The sisters spoke no more of the incident but Joan couldn't get that niggling feeling out of her mind. The feeling that she'd had when she had first spoken to the girl on that stormy night, only two days before. She knew that the other sisters fully accepted that the girl was who she said she was, but the question still lay in Joan's troubled heart — what was her real name? She drew a deep breath and prepared to go upstairs to the guest room to tell Mary that lunch was ready, just as if the incident had never happened. What would Mary's reaction be? The girl would be expecting anger and Joan was only human — she was very angry. Their lives had been upset by this wanderer. She had enough to worry about already, hadn't she? But there was something about this girl that brought a protective feeling into her soul. At all costs she would follow her vocation and care for this child — whether the girl wanted it or not. As she went up the stairs she sighed and thought, Oh, Mary Winter! — who are you?

CHAPTER SEVEN

By the time she reached the third step of the stairs, Sister Joan, Mother Superior of the Stella Maris Convent, didn't feel very superior at all. She was shaking with anger, her knees felt weak and her shoulders felt as if a heavy burden was upon them. Please Lord, she thought, give me the strength and the words to do and say the right thing when I get to Mary's room. Please don't let her bar the door against me. You sent her to us out of the storm on Friday night, it's only Sunday morning and already she's caused confusion and distress. Give me a hand for the next ten minutes, please. She went up the remainder of the stairs, walked across the landing and tapped lightly on the door of the guest room. There was no reaction — no sound at all. 'Mary are you there?'

It seemed like an eternity before a small voice said, 'Yes.'

'May I come in?'

'Yes.'

Sister Joan opened the door and went into the room. Mary was sitting hunched up on the bed, her knees drawn up to her chin and her arms wrapped around them. She was wearing items of the nuns' spare clothing because her own things had been soaked in the rain and she looked like a small tight grey bundle. Her long blonde hair scrunched up on top of her head with the bright red bulldog clip seemed like a decoration on a sadly wrapped gift package. Her eyes were swollen with tears. Joan's anger subsided a little when she saw her.

'You're going to chuck me out now, aren't you?' Mary's lower lip trembled.

'I don't know what to do.' Sister Joan sat on the end of the bed.

'I bet the others want me out. I went right over the top down there. They won't want me here now!'

'Well, they're only human Mary, that was our only little radio. The television went blank ages ago and we couldn't afford a new one. I wouldn't be telling the truth if I said they weren't angry. I'm cross too. It was a particularly stupid and mindless thing to do. I hadn't expected that of you and, quite frankly, I'm disappointed! I imagine it was the announcement on the radio — that's why you reacted in that way wasn't it?'

Mary sniffed and rubbed her eyes with the cuff of the grey cardigan. 'Yes,' she said, almost in a whisper.

'Was it about you?'

'Yes, it was.'

'And the boyfriend — they mentioned a boyfriend? You were alone when I found you. What's that all about then?'

'Don't know anything about him.'

'You must — they said that he went missing on Friday too.'

'I don't know what he's doing — or where he is.'

'Then there is a boyfriend?'

There was a long silence. Mary straightened her legs out on the bedspread and leaned back on the pillows. 'Yes — there was a boyfriend; I don't even want to think about him.'

Sister Joan sighed. 'Talk to me, Mary. I can't decide what to do until you talk to me.'

'If you're planning to tell the police, I can tell you truthfully that I'm not a criminal — I've done nothing against the law. Apart from Mum wanting me found, the police just won't be interested. She's probably told them she's afraid for my safety and that maybe I've been kidnapped or worse. But she's just in a panic because there are things in which we're both involved, personal commitments for which I'm partly responsible, but if the others want you to get rid of me I'll go now — won't take me long to get away from here. You don't have to be bothered with me any more!' She got off the bed. 'Are my clothes dry yet?'

'Yes, your things are dry and Sister Clare has ironed them and put them in the airing cupboard.'

'Not my jeans — has she ironed them sideways? There's not supposed to be sharp creases in jeans!'

Sister Joan was amazed that Mary could think of such things after what had happened in the kitchen. She felt like calling her an ungrateful little minx, but realizing how stressed the girl was she decided to say nothing. Something seemed to compel her to make sure that Mary didn't run. She still felt the need to help her in whatever way she could. She saw panic in Mary's eyes — but she also observed truth. It was like looking into the eyes of a child who was afraid of an imagined monster — and, thought Sister Joan, monsters have no place in this house. Whatever it was they would face it together.

'Sister Clare has cooked chicken for lunch

today.' She changed the subject pointedly. 'Bill Murray up at the farm brought us a couple of birds on Friday afternoon. He said they were surplus to requirements, but we all know it was a gift — he always puts it like that. I'd be pleased if you'd join us — it's nearly ready.'

Mary looked incredulous, but Joan could see that she was shaking. 'You're so unreal — all of you,' she said. 'Why are you being so nice?'

Sister Joan put her hand on Mary's shoulder. 'You shall stay with us. If the police do have a reason to come here looking for you, then we will have to admit that you're here, we would never flout the law. However, we will support you to the best of our ability. I don't want you to run any further, Mary. After all, where on earth would you go? You didn't even know where you were going when I found you, did you now? We'll all calm down and have a good lunch. Maybe later you'll feel like talking to us, or just we two on our own if you like.'

'You're not going to throw me out then? I promise you, all I want is time to sort myself out — a bit of peace. Please help me.'

'There is one condition. You really want to stay, don't you?'

'Yes, yes, I do. I feel safe here.'

85

'Then, here and now, before one morsel of Sister Clare's roast chicken passes your lips, you're going to phone your parents.'

'Oh no — oh no I'm not. I'm not telling them where I am. I'm over eighteen — I don't have to.'

'Dear girl, just tell them you're well and safe and that you'll make contact again soon. Your poor mother will be out of her mind with worry; she must have been, to risk involving the police when there was no need — it doesn't matter if you're of age or not, don't you understand?'

'She — she doesn't worry. . . .'

'Of course she does — she's your mother, she loves you.'

To Sister Joan's surprise Mary gave her a wry look. 'You don't know my mother.'

'The fact remains, Mary, that you must at least tell them you're alive, well — and in a safe place. That's the deal, I'm afraid, or no lunch!' she added, hoping that Mary would note the authority that she was trying hard to put into her voice. She sensed instinctively that Mary didn't believe that she would deny her lunch, but she would do so if the girl decided not to phone. She wouldn't lie to Mary but she prayed that the girl would not call her bluff.

As they looked into one another's eyes

Sister Joan felt that despite the girl's nervousness there was something about her personality that had strength. Suddenly, Mary reached for her holdall put it on the bed and rummaged around in it until she found her mobile phone.

'Hasn't anyone tried to phone you, Mary?'

'I've had it turned off all the time.' Mary switched on the phone. 'Are you going out while I do this?'

'Oh dear me no! I'm a very trusting person but I won't be able to sleep soundly until I know that your poor mother's mind is at rest. I shall certainly stay here.'

Mary smiled ruefully. 'OK, then — I'll phone home. No tricks, promise.' She pressed the buttons on the phone then held it to her ear and waited. 'I'm not doing this because of lunch,' she said. 'I'm doing it for you.'

It was so quiet in the guest room that Sister Joan could hear the ringing tone at the other end of the line. Someone answered.

'Mum — is that you . . . Mummy . . . ? Yes, it's me . . . I'm OK. . . . No, I'm not going to tell you that . . . no! I need some space . . . I can't tell you where I am, not yet. You'll think of something to tell them, you always do. . . . Well you can tell the police to stop looking for me now. . . . No! I'm safe here, really I am, I'm going now, I'll be in touch — promise . . . ! I can't help that, you'll have to make some excuse. You always know how. . . . Don't do that, a private detective won't ever find me here. . . . Can't talk any more. Bye!' Mary switched off the phone, put her hand over her face and shuddered. 'There — is that all right?' She threw the mobile into the holdall and zipped it up. 'She wouldn't use a private eye — she couldn't do that, surely. . . .'

Sister Joan got to her feet. If a private detective was to be involved, she thought, then the problem must be very serious even if it no longer involved the police. She put her hand on the girl's shoulder. 'My dear, we'll cross that bridge when we come to it — now, don't you feel better. I certainly do, even though it was a bit abrupt. At least your mother's mind will be at rest. You will phone her again — you promised?' She smiled when Mary nodded. 'Now we'll go downstairs, the sisters will be waiting.'

'Sister Joan?'

'Yes, dear?'

'My mother won't give up trying to find me, you know. It's — it's because of my responsibilities, you see. She'll do everything she can to get to me.'

'Then, don't you think it would be better if you told her where you are? Wouldn't she understand that you need a little time?'

Mary looked deep into Sister Joan's eyes and said quietly, 'No, she wouldn't.'

The mystery had not been solved but contact had been made. She and the sisters must be even more patient now. The journey down the stairs was a lot easier for Joan than the long emotional haul up.

The kitchen was deserted when they got there. 'Oh! Of course, they're in the refectory. We'd decided that as it was a special lunch and Sunday, too, we'd have it in there.' Sister Joan led the way and Mary followed quietly. What kind of mood the sisters would be in by now Joan couldn't guess, for they were very angry when she had gone upstairs to Mary's room. She opened the door and they went inside. All the sisters were there and a fire burned bright with logs in the hearth, but the crackling of the wood behind the old brass fireguard was all the sound there was. The nuns, gathered together at the far end of the table, gazed silently at Mary who turned quickly and made to go out again. Sister Joan caught her hand. 'Mary, if you want to stay you must face this moment; we are almost at a loss to know what to say to you.'

'I know very well what to be saying to her. I'm certainly not at any loss!' Sister Clare's cheeks were very pink. 'All that mess over my nice clean floor and the cups broken. You should be ashamed!'

Sister Imelda chipped in. 'And our little wireless gone for a Burton. What got into you? We've all been so kind to you, even though you've kept us in the dark about yourself.'

'You behaved like a hooligan,' said Sister Clare. 'My mother would have taken the wooden spoon to you, so she would!'

Joan felt Mary's hand tremble in hers. 'I'm sorry — I'm so sorry. It's just that I heard —' She gave Joan a look of sheer panic.

'The announcement on the radio was about Mary,' said Joan. 'She is the missing girl. She was frightened, what she did was a reaction to that fear. I have, in fact, something positive to tell you.' The nuns stood silently, their attention now on their Mother Superior. 'Mary has phoned her mother.'

'Oh Mary — that's a good girl — your parents will be so relieved.' Gentle Sister Flora came forward and gave her a hug.

'Jolly good show, girl — mind at rest and all that!' Sister Imelda patted her shoulder.

'Can't say I feel any better about the radio though!'

'There's roast potatoes and plenty of gravy — you'll need a good meal now, after the stress of a phone call that should have been made ages ago.' Sister Clare disappeared through the door in the direction of the kitchen. 'Someone come and give me a hand to bring in this food please,' she called. 'We've had enough disruption to the order of our day!' Sisters Emma and Imelda hurried after her.

'I don't know what to say.' Mary swept her long hair away from her face with a gesture of embarrassment. 'What I did — was unforgivable.'

'Imelda will sort out the radio — her brother gave her a DIY crystal set last Christmas. She'll fix it up for us and — nothing is unforgivable, child.' Sister Flora smiled.

At the mention of another radio, Sister Joan saw a fleeting expression of the old panic in Mary's face. Her name, she thought, her real name — it wasn't announced. The little radio was smashed before they heard the presenter finish. Then, as quickly as it had appeared, the look was gone. Sister Joan sighed quietly, the last thing that Mary would want them to hear was another news flash.

'You're so darned kind — the whole lot of you. I don't know how you manage it. Mum would have gone ballistic!'

'Dear child,' said Sister Flora. 'Whatever going ballistic means, after you ran upstairs most of us probably did!'

'You must have wanted to throw me out right there and then.'

Sister Flora smiled. 'Well, actually, some of us certainly wanted to. You frightened us, you know — we thought you'd gone quite mad.'

'I'm so sorry.'

Sister Joan put her arm around Mary's shoulders and led her to a place beside her own chair at the head of the table. She noticed that the girl hadn't flinched when Sister Flora had embraced her. Maybe her confidence in them was growing and she had accepted the fact that they still wanted to help her whatever the problem. 'Well it's a good start, Mary,' she said. 'You've contacted your mother and promised to keep in touch. The police will stop searching for you so we can all relax and you can sort out your troubles in your own time. After all, going missing is not an offence.' But, she thought, the effect it has on the hearts and minds of those waiting at home could be devestating. 'Now we'll have a lovely meal together, courtesy of Bill Murray and his surplus chickens,' she smiled.

'You're so kind and I feel much better.' Mary looked at Sister Joan. 'But you see, the trouble is, that my time is not really my own at all. Mum probably will put a private detective onto me for lots of reasons. My disapearance will affect a lot of people. Oh, there's tons of reasons for her to want to find me soon.'

Before Joan could ask, 'Why? Just tell me one of those reasons!' The sisters returned from the kitchen with the food and the moment had gone. She clasped her hands as they took their seats and said grace.

'My word, look at this feast — it's like Christmas and we hardly deserve it,' laughed Sister Imelda, as Clare began to carve. Sister Imelda grinned and nudged Mary with her elbow. 'Sisters Louise and Amy grew the vegetables. Four green thumbs those two have got. Whatever they plant — well, it'd better jolly grow or they'd want to know why not!'

'We must save some of this for Sister Madeline, she's due home tomorrow. I do hope her mother's better.' Sister Joan accepted the plate offered her by Clare.

'Oh, she's bound to be better,' said Sister

Imelda and, turning to Mary, 'Sister Madeline was a nurse, you know, you'll like her — jolly handy having her around. She makes you realize that you can't possibly be poorly while she's there with her possets and potions. In fact, it's better to get up and keep going rather than take some of them!'

'Now, now, Imelda. It's hardly fair to say that when Madeline isn't here to speak up for herself.' Sister Joan smiled around at them all, the meal was seasoned with their laughter and the atmosphere became a little more relaxed. She decided, however, that after lunch would be the time to tell them about the letter from the Mother House, while their spirits were calm enough to be able to absorb the news and deal with it sensibly. After all, Mary wasn't their only problem. Maybe, in a short time her troubles would be solved and she would leave, but their current worries would remain. She watched them eating and exchanging quiet conversation — there was no Rule of Silence for their Order during mealtimes or any time for that matter. This was a family. Give them strength, Lord, she prayed silently, maybe a few good ideas as well and — when she smashed the radio — forgive me for wanting to take a wooden spoon to Mary in the tradition of Sister Clare's mother!

CHAPTER EIGHT

The dishes that had contained a pudding of
stewed apples and instant custard were still
in front of them. Sister Joan hadn't been
able to wait for the table to be cleared. She
had considered asking Mary to leave the
dining-room as she had something important to tell the nuns, but that would have
made them uneasy. Mary would have noticed the change in the sisters when they
knew what the letter contained because they
would be talking about it. If she thought
she had been dismissed because they wanted
to discuss her, she would probably listen at
the door anyway, so she decided that Mary
should stay. The letter from the Mother
House weighed heavy in her heart, so immediately after the meal she told the sisters
quietly and simply the message that it contained.

'How long have you known about this?'
Sister Imelda leaned her elbows on the

refectory table and cupped her chin in her hands.

'Since Friday morning, before I went to get the MOT for Sister Ford. When the old car failed I hadn't the heart to tell you — and then I found Mary half-drowned in the lane and I just put it aside.'

'You should have told us right away, Mother. Not good to bottle up y'know — only get indigestion and sleepless nights,' said Imelda.

'I hadn't thought — about money and the roof and everything. We've always muddled along. I had no idea things had got serious.' Sister Flora sat with her hands clasped in her lap.

'A trouble shared is a trouble halved and you've got the eight of us to divide it between. With all respect, Mother, you should have told us immediately!' Clare, still seated, began to pile up the dishes as the others passed them down the table automatically.

'I told Father Anderson this morning after mass.'

'Before us?' Sister Clare sat with a plate poised above the others in the pile.

'I-I thought that maybe he'd have an answer.'

'And did he?'

'No, but he said he'd put on his thinking cap.'

'Well, now, that'll be useful when it rains!'

'Sister!'

Sister Clare put down the dish. 'Well. I feel upset. I'm sorry Mother.'

Sister Joan could see tears of frustration welling in Clare's eyes and there was a small silence as if they were all lost for words.

'Don't you get paid then, you lot? I mean, do you work at being nuns for nothing?' said Mary.

Sister Emma giggled quietly. 'We do it for love, Mary — it's called a vocation.'

Sister Joan patted Mary's hand. 'We get a little money from the Mother House but we're expected to earn some for ourselves. This is a big old house, not such a burden a hundred years ago when it was almost new, but time and the world catches up on everything sooner or later. I'm sorry Mary, this really isn't your problem; you have enough of your own. Don't worry about our troubles. You shouldn't be here listening to all this but I hadn't the heart to send you out.'

'But you've been so good to me, when I've been so awful. I've only been here a little while but — I feel so close to you. You must put up a fight to stay here!'

Sister Clare stood up. 'If the two of you on the washing-up rota will follow me we'll get these dishes done.' She picked up a stack of plates. 'The good Lord knows well what we need before we're even asking for it. Something will turn up for certain — you can be sure of that.' She made her way to the kitchen followed by her two helpers.

'You need to have a think tank,' said Mary.

'What on earth is that?' Imelda asked.

'It's when you all get together and exchange ideas. Sit around the table like we are now and say what we think ought to be done.'

Sister Joan smiled. 'We do that often, dear.'

'But we could write it down, like a proper meeting, then have a look at what everyone's said and try to come to some sort of decision.'

'Sounds like good sense — wouldn't do any harm, y'know.' Imelda glanced at Sister Joan.

'We could do it right now, this afternoon, when the others get back from the kitchen. Now would be a good time, wouldn't it?' Mary looked eagerly from face to face.

'You're very persuasive, Mary, and it is a good idea — however, I think that you should be excused from participating in this. You must feel free to spend the afternoon as you please. You mustn't get too involved in our problems. It could be that the only solution will be for us to close the house and return to headquarters for further orders. The Mother House will take care of us all whatever happens. It'll just mean starting again somewhere else. In any case, you mustn't be worried by any decision we have to make.'

'Jolly well agree with that, Mother. Brilliant idea, Mary, but we should shoulder this burden ourselves.' Sister Imelda leaned back in her chair and placed her large capable hands on the table.

'You've got to be joking! It's my idea and anyway what would happen if you had to leave and someone else nearly drowns in a storm and you're not there to help!'

'That's most unlikely, dear.' Sister Joan smiled at Mary's newly found courage. Where was the violent and frightened waif of a few hours ago?

Mary put her small hand on Joan's. 'I was most unlikely, wasn't I? But I happened just the same, didn't I? I must help if I can!'

'No, Mary, not with this.' Sister Joan was touched at the girl's concern and her eagerness to put her own troubles to one side in an attempt to help them.

Mary was silent for a while. 'You do want

the car tomorrow, don't you?' she said quietly.

'Girl's jolly well blackmailing you, Mother!' said Imelda.

Joan gave a tired sigh and thought of the scene upstairs in the guest room when she had persuaded Mary to phone her parents or go without lunch. Touché, she thought. 'Very well, Mary, we'll have your think tank and you may be included.'

Mary grinned and said, 'Wicked!'

'It means marvellous — wonderful — first rate and all that,' Sister Imelda explained before Joan could ask. 'Wicked doesn't seem to mean what it used to these days.'

The think tank, although bringing a lot of ideas together and using up even more paper than Sister Joan had thought possible, didn't sort out the problem as immediately as they had expected. Most of the ideas were for short term methods of earning money but they needed something that they could do on a permanent basis.

Mary suggested that they start a bed-and-breakfast business and make over another room to this end, but Sister Clare was a little uneasy about strangers who were not exactly in need and might be demanding.

'There's rules and regulations about that

sort of thing, you know, and we'd probably have to spend a lot of money making the place suitable to pass all sorts of tests and inspections — and we haven't got that in the first place,' she said wisely.

'But I'm staying here — and I'm going to give you some money for having me,' Mary said.

'That's different child, you've come to us in exceptional circumstances. You are what could be termed as a one-off,' Sister Imelda smiled.

Sisters Amy and Louise suggested that they sell gardening tips to the local paper and that was written down in the 'good idea' column.

'We could maybe do a book about growing strange vegetables,' Amy said shyly. 'But that would take more than a year, provided the publishers liked it, and what with photos and everything, it would be too late — and I wouldn't know where to send it anyway.'

They sat around the refectory table all the afternoon, sharing ideas and writing them down. The think tank accompanied them to tea and long into the evening.

On Monday morning as she sat at the desk in her study and tapped the papers together, fastening them with a paper clip, Sister Joan suddenly felt a lot more confident about their situation. Somehow it was better now that all of them knew. She wrote a letter of acknowledgement to the Mother House, put the copy with the think tank papers and placed them all in the top drawer which she kept as her 'immediate' file. They would fight this together. She felt sure they would win and that something would happen that would enable them to stay in the old house — if not, well, they would have given it a jolly good try. As Sister Clare had said: the Lord knows what you need before you even ask for it.

Mary appeared dressed in her own clothes at lunchtime and blushed when Sister Clare smiled and said, 'You see, I did iron your jeans flat, Mary — we're not so far removed from the world that we don't know about sharp creases being a no-no.' She glanced at Sister Joan and smiled. 'Bill Murray's daughter came down here with the milk the other day, all up in arms because her mother had ironed creases into her jeans. I hadn't forgotten. I'd already pressed them in the acceptable way before Sister Joan came quietly to tell me. All the young people have flat jeans now, I believe. Jill Murray tells me the pop groups especially have them like that.'

'I suppose they do. Thank you very much, Sister,' Mary said quietly.

'Would you like to come with us this afternoon, Mary? Sister Flora's appointment is at four-thirty. Maybe there are a few things you need at the shops.' Sister Joan felt sure that the girl would say yes, she was so much more relaxed than she had been two days ago.

'I-I don't think I will, thanks.' Suddenly the old nervousness had come back.

'But the police won't be searching for you now.' Sister Imelda spread low-fat margarine on her bread. 'And there's no reason why you shouldn't be staying here with us anyway.'

Mary was quiet, then she said, 'I've got no shoes, my other sandal — it's still lost. The shoes you lent me are — a bit big.'

'Leave Mary to make up her own mind. I'm sure she'd come if she really wanted to. Maybe another time,' Sister Joan said.

'Oh, yes, another time, that would be fine.' Mary concentrated on her plate, but Joan noticed that she took only a couple of bites of toast before she pushed it aside.

'That's not enough to feed a sparrow!' Clare said. 'Have a bowl of porridge, child.'

'No, no thank you,' Mary said. She got up, quickly left the table and the kitchen

104

and went upstairs to her room with not another word.

Sister Joan frowned and shook her head almost imperceptibly at the nuns — that was enough. The sisters understood. Mary still needed very gentle handling.

CHAPTER NINE

'Here are the keys and there's some money for petrol. Do drive carefully, Sister — she's very powerful.' Mary passed over the keys on an extra large and colourful keyring and some folded notes to Sister Imelda. 'Are you sure you can manage?'

'Oh, yes! Driven most things in my jolly lifetime — no problem. I'll get the feel of her as we go up the lane. By the time we've reached the highway we'll be well away!' Sister Imelda held the door open so that Sisters Joan and Flora could get into the back. Then, closing it, she opened the driver's door and eased herself into the seat. 'Bit of a tight fit, but we'll manage. Don't you worry, I'll bring everyone back all in one piece — except for the jolly tooth, of course,' she laughed.

The motor purred as soon as she turned the key in the ignition and after a rather spectacular start which resulted in a spray of gravel all over the front doorstep, they made their way up past the wrought-iron gates and into the lane. Sister Joan breathed more easily as Imelda gradually took control and they made their way carefully onto the main road.

'Better not go to Len Harvey's for the petrol. Mary still seems a bit jumpy about the car being seen. Anyway, I don't think we've got enough fuel to get that far. I syphoned the last drop out of Sister Ford's tank before we left so we should just make it to that new service station before town. It's a self-service one, so they won't take any notice of the car.'

Sister Imelda was wrong. The girl in the garage was busy filing her nails when Sister Imelda went to pay for the petrol, but she looked out onto the forecourt through the window by the till and Joan could see that she was asking something. Sister Imelda made her way back to the car and eased herself into the driver's seat.

'What did the girl say, I saw her looking?' Joan said.

'Oh, she asked me if I was a nun and I said "Yes", and then she said "Posh car!" and I said "Someone lent it to us", and she said "Lucky you!" and all I could think of saying was, "The Lord provides!" '

The car was warm and comfortable and Imelda was driving carefully but the girl's words made Joan begin to feel a little conspicuous as they neared town.

It was almost dark by the time they reached Mr Macpherson's surgery. There was a light over his nameplate beside the door and Sister Joan felt Flora tremble a little as they pulled up outside.

'It'll be over very soon, my dear, and we'll all be home again.' Sister Joan squeezed Flora's hand. 'Imelda will stay with you all the time, won't you, Sister?'

'Jolly well won't leave her side.' Imelda turned to look at them. 'That's if I can get myself out of this seat again.'

Sister Joan smiled. Imelda could always cheer them up. Flora laughed and of course she could get out of the car. She opened the door for them and Joan looked at her watch. 'We're right on time — well done, Sister.'

'Have you got Sister Clare's shopping list, Mother?' Imelda took Sister Flora's arm.

'Yes, I thought I'd go and do that while you're in the surgery. The supermarket isn't far. I should be back before you're finished and then we can get home again.'

Although it was nearly dark Sister Joan still felt uneasy about the car. Mary had convinced her that she was in no trouble as far as the police were concerned, but there were other reasons for her to hide and until she confided in them they must respect those. As she walked down the road towards the supermarket it suddenly occured to her how strange they must look, three nuns in a bright red Porsche. She rehearsed in her head what she would say if PC Bradley came round the corner or Len Harvey: Oh, we have a guest staying with us, she generously lent us the car. That would do. But a Porsche — a visitor in a Porsche? People with that sort of car stayed in expensive hotels, not crumbling off-the-beaten-track convents. She began to wish that she'd asked Bill Murray for a lift after all. Three nuns zooming around like pop stars in such a car might not be approved of by the Mother House. She caught her breath; were there double yellow lines outside Mr Macpherson's? What if they got a parking ticket? She turned and looked back, thinking that if the lines were there, and PC Bradley noticed and gave them a parking ticket, how would she explain that to her superiors? There were none and she breathed a sigh of relief. Sister Imelda would have noticed anyway, wouldn't she?

The supermarket was a small one and the

staff knew the nuns and the Stella Maris Convent very well. Sister Joan went around the shelves. Porridge for breakfast — maybe a crunchy-nut honey cereal for Mary. She didn't seem to fancy porridge although Sister Clare said it would do her the world of good. 'Poor thin little thing, she's nought but a crease in the sheets,' Clare had whispered to Joan. Sliced bread, margarine, marmalade, flour and sugar. Eggs came from their own chickens and milk courtesy of Bill Murray's cows who pleaded a surplus every other day. Thinking of Mary, Joan slipped a bar of chocolate into the trolley, she'll enjoy that; cheer her up a bit.

One of the staff was setting up a display of the latest CD with an enormous poster of the singer, a girl, dressed in what appeared to be nothing more than a silver petticoat and shoes with heels in which no ordinary mortal could hope to walk comfortably. Her make-up was bizarre to say the least. Mary would like that, thought Sister Joan, in fact the girl looked a bit like Mary, but that was the image to which most young girls aspired nowadays. She wheeled her trolley to the end of the queue at the till and waited her turn.

'We'll deliver this shall we, Sister?' The checkout girl smiled at her.

'Oh, yes please, that would be kind.' They always delivered but it was nice to make a little conversation.

'Everyone well up at the convent?' the checkout girl bleeped the items past the computerized till.

'Oh yes all very well. Sister Flora is having a tooth out at this moment up at Mr Macpherson's, but that will be a relief for her.'

'Oh! Poor love, but sometimes it's better out than in,' said the girl without taking her eyes off the labels.

'Indeed, yes,' said Joan.

'This fruit and nut yours?' The girl held up the chocolate. 'Only you don't have that kind of thing usually, do you? What about the crunchy-nut flakes, yours too?'

'We have a visitor staying with us,' Joan said with a smile. 'I thought she'd like some little treats.'

'Oh, you are a love,' said the girl. 'Something special for the guest. Nuns are all kindness, aren't they?' She smiled at the lengthening queue.

'Thank you, my dear, we try to be.' Joan handed her the money.

'We'll get your groceries along to you soon as we can — this evening anyway. Tell Sister Flora good luck and I hope the toothache

111

will be better now.' She tore the receipt from the till and handed it to Sister Joan with the change. 'Thank you, 'bye! Next one please!'

It was quite dark when she went outside and the air struck cold in comparison with the over-warmth of the supermarket. Before her eyes became accustomed to the gloom she almost bumped into someone.

'Why! Reverend Mother you got into town after all. Sister Flora at the dentist's then?' Len Harvey's lined face grinned at her. 'Bill Murray give you a lift?'

Joan was startled. The speech she had prepared went completely out of her head. 'I — we got a lift. . . .'

'Oh yes?' Len Harvey's question was still there to be answered.

'We have a visitor — she lent us her car.'

'Well now, the Lord provides, don't he? Sister gonna be all right?'

'I'm sure she will, thank you so much for asking. I must hurry. They'll be out of the surgery by now.'

'Oh, yes, mustn't keep you.' Len raised his hand in a goodbye salute and walked past.

'Goodnight, Len,' Joan called, feeling a little mean to have made the conversation so abrupt.

'Oh, Reverend?'

She turned. 'Yes, Mr Harvey?'

'What kind of car is it? Only I saw a red Porsche outside Mr Macpherson's surgery. Not that one is it?' he laughed.

'Yes, actually, it is.'

'Well now, what a thrill for Sister Imelda. I gather she's driving — she wouldn't want to miss out on a treat like that. Bet she's had her head under the bonnet already, eh? Comfortable ride, ain't they, them Porsches?'

'A very comfortable car, thank you,' she replied.

He smiled. 'That's all right then. Tell Sister Imelda to take it careful, them sort of cars is a bit lively; don't want to be pullin' you all out of a ditch with me breakdown truck later on. By the way, I'm still on the lookout for a little run-around for you. You can't be without a car livin' out in the sticks like you do. We'll sort out a price when the time comes, eh? Goodnight.' He waved a cheerful farewell and continued on up the High Street.

'Goodnight, Mr Harvey,' she called, 'and thank you.'

Sister Joan pulled the collar of her coat up around her neck on the way back to the car as the wind was now against her and there

113

was a bite of ice in it. Sisters Flora and Imelda were already inside and Joan could see that Sister Flora was holding a bundle of tissues over her mouth. Sister Imelda was sitting in the driving seat. She must have seen Joan approaching for she got out and opened the door for her so that she could escape the chill wind. Sister Flora's eyes looked large above the tissues.

'My dear Sister, how was it?' Sister Joan settled down in the seat beside her.

There was a little whimper from Flora so Imelda answered for her. 'Popped out like a pea from a pod. Brave soldier she was, dentist said so. She has to keep the cold out of her mouth or she might get a bit of trouble. Got plenty of painkillers, Mr Macpherson gave us some. Better get home soon as poss.' She eased herself into the driving seat. 'Home in a brace of shakes, Sisters.'

'Not too fast, Imelda. Better to arrive safe than sorry,' Joan said as she helped Sister Flora with her seat belt.

'Look what I found while we were waiting for you.' Sister Imelda pressed a button and the glovebox opened. 'Lots of CDs — I thought there must be a player in here somewhere and I found it. Shall we have some music?'

'Do you think we should? It is Mary's property you know,' Joan was reluctant to share Imelda's excitement.

' 'Course she won't mind. Look, I've already worked out how to use it — jolly simple really.' She took a CD from its pack and placed it in the player. 'Look at the picture on the front of this, Sisters. Poor girl would catch her death walking around dressed like that. Let's see what Mary likes to listen to.' She pressed a button, turned the key in the ignition and they drove away from Mr Macpherson's surgery to the very latest recording by the girl in the silver petticoat and outrageous shoes that Joan had seen in the supermarket.

'It's a bit loud Imelda, do you think you can turn it down a bit,' Sister Joan said, conscious of the attention they might be attracting.

'Control should be here somewhere.' Imelda fumbled with the buttons on the dashboard.

Sister Joan closed her eyes and remembered Len Harvey's warning to go carefully.

The darkness seemed to close around them as they left the bright lights of the main highway and turned into the lane that led to the convent. Sister Imelda slowed the

Porsche down. The car was warm, they had made it to the dentist and back with no mishap and — apart from a few turned heads at the loud music — without attracting too much attention, Sister Joan felt relaxed and safe. They went in through the open iron gates and approached the front door.

Imelda stopped the Porsche. 'Shall I drop you off here, Mother?'

'No, we'll put the car away first and tuck it up safely. It was kind of Mary to lend it to us; we must do that first. Are the barn doors open?'

'Yes.'

'We'll put Mary's car on the other side of Sister Ford and cover it with that old tarpaulin to keep the dust off. You won't mind walking to the house will you, Flora? Just keep the tissues over your mouth.'

'I'll walk to windward of you, Flora,' Imelda said. 'Shelter you from the icy blast!'

Sister Flora's eyes crinkled at the corners as she smiled under the tissues.

Imelda cruised the car slowly across the driveway and into the barn, parking it neatly as Joan had suggested.

'Oh, she drives like a dream,' she said. 'I hope I can have another go soon.'

Joan and Imelda got out, found the tar-

116

paulin and, handling it between them, draped it over the car.

'There now,' Sister Joan said. 'That's all safe and sound. Let's get indoors out of this wind.' Suddenly a frantic tapping came from inside the car.

'Oh dear — oh lumme! We've left Flora inside, poor dear!' Imelda lifted the tarpaulin to reveal a grey veil and two wide and frightened eyes at the side window, the tissues still held obediently to her mouth. 'Hold on, Sister, have you out in a jiffy — I do apologize and all that!'

After closing and padlocking the big barn doors they made their way to the house and went inside. The sound of gentle laughter came from the kitchen.

They took off their coats and hung them in the big cupboard in the hall. Warmth and the smell of fresh baked scones enveloped them as Sister Joan opened the kitchen door. Mary and Emma were sitting at the table, and Sister Clare was putting strawberry jam on a scone.

'Well now, you're home, all of you, all safe and sound, thank God.' Sister Clare beamed at them. 'Ah, the toothache is a nasty thing, but it's over now. Flora, come and sit here, was it terrible? You poor soul and I don't suppose you can eat a thing. Here I'll find a straw and you can have some milky tea.'

Flora took the tissues away from her face and gave a little sigh. 'I'm feeling much better now, thank you,' she managed to say.

'Wonderful car, Mary, I did enjoy driving it. Thank you so much for lending it to us,' Sister Imelda enthused.

'Oh, that's OK,' Mary said. 'It's the least I could do.'

'We took the liberty of playing one of your CDs on the way home — found 'em in the glovebox, worked out how to use the jolly player. Strange songs though — I didn't understand a word of any of them,' she laughed.

There was a silence. Sister Joan saw that Mary wasn't smiling. 'Which one did you play?' she asked.

'Oh, I just picked up the first to hand, didn't sort 'em out. Girl on the front with half a frock on and heels like stilts. Cheered us up on the way home though. I did put it all back tidy,' she added. 'Hope you don't mind.'

' 'Course not,' Mary said. 'Those CDs — they're a bit noisy and modern for you. Sometimes they sound like a lot of noise to me, too, but people seem to buy that sort of stuff — including me,' she grinned.

Sister Joan smiled. 'I think we turned

quite a few heads this evening. It was quite an adventure.'

'By the way, here are your keys, Mary.' Imelda handed them over. 'I've never seen such a big keyring, not likely to lose that are you? Oh, look, I didn't notice it before, there's a picture of that girl in the silver frock, the one we were listening to in the car. What's on the back?' Imelda turned over the picture on the keyring. 'Oh, yes, "Becky-Marie — Gucci Foot". Must be her name, didn't notice it on the CD pack. Should be your name and address on it, Mary, it's your keyring.' Imelda laughed. 'If you lost it how would it ever be returned to you?'

Mary took it and said. 'The thing is, Sister, if my name and address were on it and I lost it, then someone could steal the car. But I do take great care of my keys. I'm glad you enjoyed driving it. You must have another go soon. Did you put it back in the barn?'

'Yes, she's all safe and sound. Tucked up beside old Sister Ford.'

'You're very kind, Sisters.' Mary put the keys into the back pocket of her jeans.

The kitchen was warm and filled with the smell of baking and the sounds of friendly conversation. Sister Joan felt relaxed and happy that Flora was out of pain. The colour was beginning to return to her cheeks as she drank her milky tea through a straw left over from the summer church fête. The name on the keyring kept coming into Joan's mind: was it just an advertisement for the recording, a bit of publicity? Or was Becky-Marie Mary's real name? It couldn't be — she was just feeling tired. It was a silly name anyway — Gucci Foot!

Mary was the first to hear the sound of a car coming up the driveway. 'Listen!' She jumped to her feet. 'Who's that?'

'Probably the groceries,' Joan said. 'They said they'd deliver them sometime this evening.'

As the car pulled up outside, Sister Clare moved over to the window and they all joined her to look out as she pulled aside the blue curtains. The light from the front porch illuminated a white car that pulled up outside. The headlights were turned off and the driver's door opened.

'Oh dear, oh lumme!' Imelda said. 'It's not the groceries — it's the police! What in heaven's name does Constable Bradley want at this time of night?'

Chapter Ten

As soon as she caught a glimpse of PC Bradley, Mary ran out of the kitchen and up the stairs to her room almost before Sister Clare had pulled the curtains closed again. Joan heard the door of the guest-room bang shut. Young Sister Emma made to follow her but Joan held up a restraining hand.

'No, Sister! Stay here with us please,' she said quietly. 'There is absolutely no reason to panic. We have no idea yet what it is that Constable Bradley wants.' The doorbell rang. 'Sister, if you will kindly go and make him welcome I am sure we would all be grateful.' she smiled and nodded at Sister Clare, who hurried away to open the front door.

'Oh, dear, oh, lumme!' Sister Imelda sat down rather heavily on a chair at the table. 'I'll bet he saw me driving Mary's car. What if it's a stolen one after all?'

'Sisters, we have never been afraid of Constable Bradley and there is no need to be so now. The car is most certainly Mary's own and we mustn't let her reaction affect our own common sense.' Sister Joan sat down beside Imelda, patted her hand and smiled. 'If he did happen to see you driving the Porsche, my dear, you had a perfectly legitimate reason for doing so and an impeccable driving licence as well.'

'That's the truth,' Imelda said. 'And a heavy goods vehicle licence too!'

Joan smiled: 'We can explain to him that we only borrowed it from our guest to take Sister Flora to the dentist.'

Clare came back into the kitchen, her rosy face glowing with joy. 'Look who Constable Bradley has brought home safe and sound.'

Sister Madeline followed her into the room and the policeman, hat tucked neatly under his arm and carrying a plastic bag, came in last of all.

'I was on my way here,' he said, 'and I saw your sister coming out of the railway station, so I brought her home.' He smiled at them all. 'My word, it smells lovely in here, Sister Clare must have been baking something delicious.'

As the nuns gathered around to greet Sister Madeline, Clare patted the policeman on the arm. 'You're perfectly right,' she said. 'I have been baking — and if you'll take a seat you shall have a nice cup of tea and a scone.'

'With strawberry jam?' he laughed.

'Why, of course — what else?' Clare said and she began to bustle about with cups and plates.

'It's so good to have you home again.' Joan embraced Madeline. 'How is your mother?'

'I'm glad to say she's on the mend, but the flu has been awful. Even my home-made cough elixir did no good. Poor mum just couldn't stand the taste of it.'

Joan saw Sister Imelda raise her eyebrows and expected her to say something about possets and potions, but she said nothing.

'I did have another reason to come here tonight.' PC Bradley sipped his tea. 'I've been meaning to call for a couple of days, but we've been a bit busy at the station — paperwork you know.'

'What is it, Constable?' Joan sat down on the opposite side of the table.

'It's to deliver this.' He reached down beside his chair and, picking up the bag he'd been carrying, he placed it on the table. 'Chestnuts!' he said. 'Our old tree had a bumper harvest this year — wife thought you'd like some. They'll keep until Christmas. You'll have some fun roasting them on the fire.'

'Oh, how lovely,' Joan said. 'We will enjoy those. Please thank Mrs Bradley very much. I'll bet you were the one to climb up the tree though?' she laughed. 'You can never shake all of them down.'

'You're absolutely right, Reverend Mother, I certainly did!' he laughed. 'By the way, there's something else here. My headlights picked out something shiny in the mud on the side of your lane. I stopped, got out to see what it was and look what I found!'

He reached into the bag of chestnuts and drew out a strappy sandal with an outrageously high heel and a buckle decorated with something sparkly.

'Now there's a strange thing to find around here,' he said. 'Haven't found its mate, have you?'

Sister Joan gasped. 'Why, my goodness, we certainly do have the other one. It belongs to a guest who arrived on Friday evening. She-she mislaid it in the lane.'

'Mislaid it?' PC Bradley looked puzzled.

'Yes, her car ran out of petrol. She began to walk — it was dark and raining hard — she lost it.'

'Well, you'd better hang on to it then. She'll be pleased to have the both of them.

Looks expensive to me, though darned if I know how women walk in these things.'

Sister Clare held out her hand. 'Here, I'll take the grubby thing,' she said. 'I'll put it in another bag until we can give it to the owner.' She glanced at Sister Joan and rolled her eyes towards the ceiling. There was no sound from Mary in the room above.

Joan felt suddenly tired. Maybe she should tell PC Bradley all about Mary, but then, it was hardly necessary. The girl hadn't committed a crime and it was all a lot of fuss over a rather uncomfortable-looking piece of footwear. Mary would contact her mother again as she had promised, and in a few days the whole worrysome business should be sorted out. No, she wouldn't bother PC Bradley. He had enough to do, what with all the paperwork down at the station.

Sister Clare opened a door in the bottom of the dresser and took out a cardboard box in which she kept plastic bags, pieces of string, rubber bands and other items which might come in useful. She took out a bag and placing the muddy sandal inside, put it on the floor beside the dresser. 'It'll certainly need a good scrub,' she said, rinsing her fingers at the tap over the sink.

PC Bradley finished his tea. 'That was most welcome, Sisters, I must be on my way now.' He got up and, taking up his hat, he placed it under his arm. 'Thank you so much for your hospitality and I hope you enjoy the chestnuts. Keep safe, Sisters, and — if I don't see you before — have a happy Christmas.'

'You, too, and Mrs Bradley,' Joan said. 'Thank you so much for giving Sister Madeline a lift home. That was very kind.'

He turned at the door and smiled. 'No bother at all, Reverend Mother, glad to oblige. By the way, I noticed there's gravel all over your front doorstep, no doubt Bill Murray has been down here on his tractor. I noticed wide tyre marks in your lane. Best get it swept away, liable to slip on that.'

'Thank you for your concern, Constable. I'll certainly see to it.' Sister Clare accompanied him to the front door and Joan heard it close. As Clare came back into the kitchen they heard his car start and the sound of the motor gradually recede into the distance as he drove away.

Of course, Joan thought, the wheels of the Porsche were much wider than Sister Ford's and the gravel on the doorstep had been caused by Imelda's fast take-off when they began their trip to the dentist with Sister Flora. Should I have told him, she wondered, about borrowing the Porsche? Len

Harvey would probably tell him soon anyway. It would be a good story to pass on — three nuns driving around in such a vehicle. Anyway, it hardly mattered. Now Mary could have her peace and space as well as her precious sandals.

When PC Bradley had gone, Sister Madeline sat down at the table, took a sip of tea from the mug that Clare had handed her and asked, 'What guest?'

In a confusion of dialogue, interrupted occasionally by Madeline's questions, they managed to tell her all about their wanderer and the happenings over the past few days. Madeline looked exhausted when they'd finished.

'So, you've decided to shelter this strange girl, without demanding to know more or thinking what you're getting yourselves into?' She sounded quite shocked and gave a tired sigh. 'With all respect, Mother, I think that what you're doing is very dangerous and already you're all caught up in the drama of it. Although she says she's not involved in anything illegal, she could be running away from someone who could be harmful to her and therefore to us. We are eight sisters alone in a great big house in the middle of nowhere. Anything could happen.'

Joan touched her hand lightly. 'If Mary's in danger then all the more reason for us to give her shelter, Madeline.'

'Mother, please, you must think again about exactly what we're doing,' Madeline pleaded. 'Her family surely have to be informed as to her whereabouts. Although we have a vocation to serve, we also have a civic duty. The girl obviously needs help of some sort and we are not trained to cope.' She sighed. 'With respect, Mother, you could have told PC Bradley everything you know, her family would then be informed and would come to get her, and all this would have been over and done with.'

Sister Madeline was right, of course she was, Joan thought. 'But you haven't met Mary yet,' she said. 'You don't know her and we are under obligation to help those in great need. Although it's a century and a half old, that is our Rule. We must not forget that,' she added quietly.

'I think I may find the experience of getting to know Mary very interesting,' Madeline said wryly.

Sister Clare took a broom from the corner of the kitchen and thumped on the ceiling with the handle end of it. 'You can come down now,' she called. 'The policeman has gone.'

There was no sound as Mary came down the stairs. She entered the room, an over-sized grey cardigan over her tops and jeans and her feet bare. She looked so small, thin and scared, with her long hair hanging around her shoulders like a blonde veil that Sister Joan's heart went out to her.

It was obvious that Mary's old panic had returned. 'Did he want to know about me? Has someone found out I'm here? He's not coming back to get me is he?'

'There was no need to tell him anything, Mary — but we have got something for you. PC Bradley found it in the mud at the side of the lane,' Sister Clare said, as she handed Mary the small plastic bag.

'It's my other sandal, isn't it?' Mary took the bag and looked inside.

'Yes, dear. He was keen to know if we had the other one,' Joan said.

'Did you tell him you hadn't seen it?' Mary's face looked sad. 'You didn't tell lies because of me, did you?' She took the sandal out of the bag.

'Of course not, Mary, we said we had the other one. He didn't ask questions — why would he need to? Now you have the pair. You must be pleased!'

Tears welled in Mary's eyes. 'These sandals — they're so special, you don't know how glad I am to have them back. I should have gone looking for the lost one myself, but I was too scared to go out — I was terrified of being seen. Now the policeman knows they're here — if he hears anything, like mum's searching for me and there's a description, well — he's bound to come back. 'Specially if he realizes that the person they're looking for would wear things like this!' She held out the muddy sandal from one strap over her finger. Her eyes brimmed over and wet her cheeks. 'I just need some peace.' She dashed the tears away with the back of her other hand. 'And that's the one thing that Mum won't give me.'

Sister Madeline was looking with interest at Mary. Oh my, thought Joan, what now? Please Lord don't let her say anything to frighten the girl even more. We've managed to work things out between us before and have always come to amicable agreements. I don't want to pull rank on Madeline.

'Sister Clare,' said Madeline, 'some tea for Mary, I think. Our home is not a place where anyone should be afraid. Don't you agree, Reverend Mother?' She cupped Mary's little face in her hands. 'Child, you need some building up before we send you out into the world again. And tell me, how do you manage to walk around on those awful stilts?'

'With difficulty, I suppose,' chuckled Sister Imelda.

'Who are you?' asked Mary as Madeline patted her cheek.

'I'm Sister Madeline and I make sure everyone here stays healthy — with the help of Doctor Stewart, of course.'

So, Sister Joan thought, now we're all involved, even the formidable Sister Madeline, who wasted no time in sitting Mary down, taking her temperature and prescribing an early night.

'But it's always early nights here. I won't be able to sleep anyway,' protested Mary.

'Well, tonight it should be earlier.' Madeline was adamant. 'You don't look a one hundred per cent fit girl to me — too pale by far. Soon put you to rights.'

'Told you, didn't I?' whispered Sister Imelda. 'Possets and potions at the ready! Better do as she says.' She winked at Mary.

'No one's going to come looking for you, Mary, you can rest easy, you're safe here with us.' Madeline put a caring hand on Mary's shoulder. 'Now sit down and relax while I sort out a herbal tea for you.'

Joan smiled and thought that Satan himself would think twice about taking on Sister Madeline. She'd probably give him a dose of castor oil and send him packing.

It had only been three days since she had brought Mary in from the storm, half-drowned and very weak and yet it seemed as if their vocations were intended for her alone. Please let us be doing the right thing, she prayed silently. Don't let anything bad come of this.

'What was that?' Mary jumped up from her chair like a scared rabbit. 'I can hear a car coming up the drive, it's that policeman again, I know it is.' She made to run for the door and the sanctuary of her bedroom. So did Sister Emma.

CHAPTER ELEVEN

'Sister Emma! Stay right where you are, you too Mary!' Joan stood up, her hand raised a little. 'Just wait and see — it may be nothing at all. You don't have to be afraid of anything.'

They all listened — it was a motor. The vehicle stopped at the front door and after a while the bell rang.

'Oh dear, oh, lumme!' Imelda said. 'What now?'

'I'll see to it,' Clare said and disappeared into the hall. She came back smiling. 'It's only the groceries. Here,' she called back, 'bring it all into the kitchen. How kind of you to come all this way on such a dark night.'

Mary stood frozen to the spot — Joan could see that there was no escape for her. She couldn't run for the stairs because the groceries were already being carried across the hall and Sister Flora, who was not exactly sprightly, nor built for moving extra quickly, was between her and the back door. She looked at Sister Joan in panic. Joan put her finger to her lips. 'Stay calm,' she whispered.

'Put the boxes on the table, gentlemen, that will be fine.' Sister Clare cleared a space and the two young men put down the containers.

Sister Joan recognized one of them. It was Len Harvey's lad who worked at the garage as his apprentice.

'Evening, Reverend,' he said. 'Got myself a bit of part-time work at the supermarket, saving up for tickets to a pop concert in London. My favourite singer. Going on a coach we are, ain't we, Fred?'

Fred nodded. 'We're gonna see Gucci Foot — have you heard any of her CDs, Reverend?'

'I-I believe maybe we have,' Joan said, remembering the drive home from the dentist's and Sister Imelda's discovery of the CD player in Mary's car. 'How very enterprising of you. I hope you both enjoy the concert.'

'Oh yeah! Bound to be the best — can't wait, neither can Fred — can you, Fred?'

Fred smiled shyly. 'Can't wait,' he said.

'Gucci Foot! Why — that's the girl on

Mary's keyring,' Imelda said. 'She's a very noisy pop star.'

'Yeah!' said Fred. 'She's the loudest — that's why we like her.'

Len Harvey's lad looked around the kitchen. 'Ain't never been in here before — nice 'n' warm.' Rubbing his hands together, he saw Mary and grinned. 'You must be the visitor what Mr Harvey was on about. He met the Reverend in the High Street, couldn't work out how she'd got there, what with no MOT and the old car so sick. Nice of you to lend them yours — bloomin' Porsche, eh?' he grinned.

Mary blanched and said quietly, 'Yes, it's a red one.'

The boy laughed. 'Hey, Fred — just like a woman eh? Never interested in the make or year, just so long as it goes and it's the right colour!'

Fred giggled. 'Just so long as it goes — right colour,' he echoed.

'Where did a nice girl like you get a car like that then?' Len Harvey's lad winked at Mary.

It was the direct question that Joan had not yet had the courage to ask.

Mary took a step forward. 'It-it was a present for my birthday,' she answered.

'Lucky old you,' said Len Harvey's lad,

looking her up and down with appreciation. 'Got a rich dad, have you?'

Mary smiled; she looked not so frightened. After all, thought Joan, these were her contemporaries.

'Something like that,' she said, and flicked her long hair back from her face.

'Come on now, you cheeky boys.' Sister Clare laughed and ushered them to the door. 'I'm sure you've got a lot more deliveries to do.'

'Sure have,' said Fred. 'Work 'ard we do.' He turned and looked at Mary. 'You remind me of someone, did you go to school around here?' he asked.

'Come on, Fred, leave off. The lady's here for a bit of quiet. Maybe she's gonna join up with them.' He smiled at Joan. 'Fred's got a strange way of chatting up the birds.' He laughed as they both left the room.

'Do we have a bird then? Where in heaven's name did that come from?' Sister Flora sounded puzzled.

'It's just an expression, dear,' explained Joan. 'It means girl.'

'Young people — it's a whole new language these days,' Flora sighed.

Joan heard the front door close and Clare came back into the kitchen. There was silence in the room until the sound of the delivery van died in the distance.

'You told somebody about me.' Mary said it quietly but Sister Joan knew it was a challenge. 'I thought you'd let me stay here and no one would know. I felt safe. Why did you do that?' Although her face was pale and her hand shook as she brushed her long hair away from her face, her voice was calm.

'I only said that we had a visitor. Len Harvey wanted to know how we got into town. He knew he'd failed our car's MOT because it's an old bucket of bolts with no life left in it. He just wanted to know if we'd got a lift from Bill Murray up at the farm and he'd seen the Porsche anyway, outside the dentist's. He was amused when I told him that Sister Imelda was driving it. I didn't have to tell him your name. He just knows we have a guest. Would that be so unusual?'

'I suppose not — I'm sorry.'

'Oh, please, don't be sorry — it's hard for all of us to understand why you're so secretive, but we're all agreed that you should stay until you're ready for us to help you sort out your problem,' Joan said.

'Actually,' said Sister Imelda, 'we haven't had a visitor for yonks — it is a bit unusual, but it's jolly exciting.'

'Oh, yes,' said Sister Emma, her cheeks

pink against the grey veil. 'Very exciting.'

Sister Madeline put her hand on Mary's shoulder. 'Bed, my girl, before another moment passes. Have you had something to eat?'

'Yes, thanks, Sister Clare cooked something for me while the others were at the dentist's. I-I suddenly felt too hungry to wait for supper.'

'Good girl — that's what you need: plenty of sleep, fresh air and good food. You'll be ready to conquer the world in a few days. Go up to bed now and I'll bring you some camomile tea.'

Sister Imelda leaned towards Mary and whispered, 'See? Told you she puts everyone to rights, but she means well despite her possets and potions.'

Sister Madeline smiled and raised her eyebrows slightly. 'I heard that, Imelda,' she said.

Sister Joan peeped into Mary's room on her way to bed. As far as she knew there had been no repeat of the nightmares that she had witnessed in the early morning of the first day that the girl had been with them. No sound had come from the guest room as the nuns filed past and down the stairs to the chapel for morning prayers each day after that.

Joan slept soundly and only woke when Sister Clare put her head around the door and said quietly, 'Good morning — God bless you.'

She washed, dressed, joined her sisters on the landing and led them quietly down the stairs to morning prayers.

The chapel struck cold as they entered and Joan switched on the light.

'Jolly boiler's gone on the blink again!' whispered Sister Imelda as she eased herself into her place in the pew beside Joan. 'I shall go into battle with it directly after breakfast.'

After the morning prayers and hymns they rose and left their pews to go to the kitchen. At least the Rayburn would have warmed that room. To her surprise Joan noticed that a chair by the chapel door was occupied. It was Mary, sitting in her borrowed nightie and dressing gown, with the eiderdown wrapped around her.

'Why, Mary! Couldn't you sleep? Did we wake you up? We try not to disturb you in the morning.'

'Couldn't sleep any more — went to bed too early. I heard you singing so I came down. You don't mind, do you?'

'Of course not, dear — you're very welcome to join us at any time, you know that. We're going to breakfast now, would you like some?'

'No, thank you, not now. I-I feel as if I'd like to go back to bed for a while. Then I must scrub the mud off my sandals. It's important for them to be nice and clean.'

The blessed sandals again, thought Joan. What could be so important about those ugly things. 'You look very pale, Mary,' she said. 'Why don't you stay in bed this morning. Sister Clare will bring you something a little later.'

Mary got up from the chair and pulled the eiderdown more closely around her shoulders. She shivered. 'Yes, thank you. I think I'll do just that.' She made her way across the hall to the stairs, the hem of the dressing gown dragging on the floor behind her, and walked slowly up to her room.

Joan watched her with concern. Even though it was so early the girl wasn't just sleepy. She was lethargic. Something is not quite right, she thought. I'm so very glad that Madeline is home.

CHAPTER TWELVE

'There's something wrong with that girl,' said Sister Madeline at lunch time. 'She's a bad colour for a young lady of her age. She should be bright as a button and full of the joys of life.'

'We don't know yet what she's been through or is going through,' Joan said. 'We have to be patient and wait until she tells us — and then, we must help all we can regardless of what the mystery is.'

'She hardly touched the breakfast I took up to her this morning. Just ate the orange that I'd put on the tray as an afterthought. It would have been such a waste of all those nutty flakes if Imelda hadn't finished them up.' Clare stirred the soup pot and the savoury smell filled the room.

'Waste not, want not,' said Sister Imelda.

'Young girls are always watching their weight,' said Madeline, 'but no doubt she'll have double helpings at lunch. However, I

141

don't like the look of her. Maybe we should get the doctor to come and see her.'

'She'd really panic if we did that,' Imelda said. 'Wouldn't see her for jolly dust!'

'All this cloak and dagger stuff makes it very difficult for us to do anything for her at all,' said Madeline.

As Sister Flora took the soup bowls from the dresser the back door opened and let in a gust of cold air.

'Oh, Mary! There you are! My dear child, we didn't know you were up and out in the garden. Are you feeling better now? You looked so peaky this morning.' Sister Joan helped her remove the large purple anorak that belonged to Sister Imelda.

'Yes, thanks, I think I was just sleepy. I've been having a look around. I found my car in the barn. Thank you for covering it up.' She slipped off the over-large borrowed shoes and, leaving them on the doormat, came into the room in thick grey woollen socks pulled up over the legs of her jeans.

'Did you walk down to the shore?' Sister Emma pulled out a chair for her.

'No, it's a bit far. There might have been someone down there.' She sat down and looked around at them all. 'They've found — they've found Allan, my boyfriend.' She sat quietly, her hands spread out on the table, waiting for someone to speak.

'Mary?' Sister Joan put her hand over the girl's cold fingers. 'How do you know this?'

Mary's face was expressionless. It was impossible for Joan to understand what the girl was feeling. 'Car radio. It was on the news just now,' Mary said. 'The search for him has been called off.'

'The car radio — I never thought of that!' said Imelda. 'And there I was driving the thing. Got a dashboard like Concorde that Porsche — never would have found the right button anyway. Poor old Sister Ford's wireless has been out of order for so long, I sort of got used to it not being there.'

'There's something else,' sighed Mary. 'My mother was on the radio after the news — there was a message in case I was listening. She's hired a private detective.'

'Well, now,' Sister Madeline said. 'Your mother must be a person of some consequence to be able to persuade the BBC to let her send you a message.'

Sister Joan noted a tone of disbelief in Madeline's voice and there was a long silence before the girl answered.

'They let anyone send a message if they think it's important enough.' Mary was on the defensive. 'I-I'm going to phone Mum again later.'

'And you — are you important?' Madeline's question was deceptively gentle.

'She — Mum has her reasons — I'm her daughter. She she loves me!' Mary's cheeks were brighter than Joan had ever seen.

'But I understood that she didn't care — wouldn't give you any peace if she found out you were here.' Sister Madeline continued to probe.

Joan could see tension in Mary's back and shoulders. The girl removed her hands from the table slowly and clenched them in her lap. Joan recognized the signs — Mary was preparing to run. Oh, Madeline, please be careful, she thought.

'It's none of your business anyway,' Mary said quietly.

'Well, now,' answered Madeline. 'And here I was thinking it was everyone's business — putting special messages and "gone missing" reports on the radio and all of us looking after you and giving you shelter.'

There was a silence. Their eyes met and held over the table.

'I think that will be enough for now, Sister.' Joan broke the silence and brought blessed relief to the situation. 'Mary — it's wonderful that your boyfriend has been found and the search for him has been called off,' she smiled.

Mary turned to face her. 'Yes, it's good news, I suppose, although I don't ever want to see him again, but if the private detective traces me as far as the town, he'll go straight to see your policeman and he'll probably put two and two together and tell the man where he suspects I'm staying. Private eyes have usually been in the police force — there'll be an old-school-tie network.'

'You seem to know a lot for a girl of your tender years, Mary — about the world.' Madeline, disregarding Sister Joan's request for their conversation to come to an end, smiled knowingly.

Mary glowered but didn't reply and Joan felt uneasy. It was becoming obvious at this moment that Mary didn't like Sister Madeline one little bit. The girl was beginning to show a strength that none of them had seen before. A quiet control that was not in any way like the behaviour of the girl who had smashed their little radio so violently. Madeline, accustomed to investigating symptoms, was revealing another side of Mary and Joan felt that it was far too soon for such a confrontation.

'Sister, I think that really is enough,' she said firmly.

'As you wish, Mother.' Sister Madeline inclined her head towards her superior.

'Soup's ready!' Sister Clare's soft Irish voice cleared the atmosphere.

'Lovely!' said Imelda. 'I'm just ready for that.'

'I think, maybe, we all are,' Joan said quietly. She looked forward to an afternoon of paperwork and solitude.

Sister Joan looked at the diary for the rest of the week. Madeline would be busy. At least three people in the district who were elderly and lived alone had flu or heavy colds. Sister Madeline would visit them, trundling along the lanes and the main road on her bicycle, which was kept in well-oiled and rust-free condition by Sister Imelda. Doctor Stewart never gave Madeline care of patients who were too far afield. Sometimes she would stay with a sick and lonely person all night, just sitting beside them and tending to their needs. The doctor called her his Angel of Mercy. Imelda maintained, however, that because of Sister Madeline's bag of home remedies, her patients probably thought it wise to get better a lot quicker than the others who were beyond her territory. There was a light tap on the door of Joan's study. 'Come in.'

'Can I talk to you, Sister?' It was Mary. She entered, closed the door behind her, crossed the room and sat down on a chair in front of the large oak desk.

'Of course you may talk to me, child. What is it?' she said.

'You know I asked you if I could stay longer?'

'Yes, dear.'

'Well, I'd like to stay a week or two if that's all right.' She put an envelope on the desk. 'There's some money in there to cover my costs for a fortnight. I wouldn't want you and the sisters to go without to feed me.'

'But, Mary — there's no need. . . .'

'Yes, there is. If I'd got further in the car I would be staying at a quiet little hotel somewhere. I'd have had to pay for that and probably more for them to keep quiet about me and I wouldn't have had such TLC so I think it's only fair that I pay you for having me. Can I stay that long?'

'Well, of course you can, dear.' Sister Joan picked up the envelope and opened it. The colour rushed to her cheeks. It was more cash than she had seen for a long, long time. 'This is far too much,' she gasped.

Mary smiled. 'You're a bit out of touch with things, Sister. That's what it'd cost if I was staying somewhere else. Believe me — I know. Please take it and don't spend it on

147

posh food — I'm happy to muck in with you and the sisters. I'm just grateful to have the peace and quiet to — to sort things out. Is that OK?'

Joan was still almost speechless. 'Well, yes, that's much more than just OK. Thank you, Mary.'

Mary got up from the chair. 'That's all I wanted, Sister — except. . . .'

'Yes, dear?'

'Can you keep Sister Madeline off my back for a while, until I'm sorted?'

'I can't promise that. Sister Madeline is a very caring person and only wants the best for you as do we all. However, I'll ask her not to be so — so searching in her approach to you. Will that suffice?'

Mary grinned, said 'Wicked!', and left the room.

Now I know what wicked means, thought Joan, but I'll have to ask Sister Imelda about TLC.

She had been too polite to count the money while Mary was in the room but she counted it now — and then again. Her hands were shaking. The boiler — we can get the boiler fixed, she thought, and the electricity bill — we can actually pay it on time. Suddenly a little sunshine beamed into her life. Then reality took over. How did Mary come to have access to such a lot of money? Where did she get it? Joan knew that she was, maybe, a little out of touch with the world but she did know that it was rare indeed for someone to carry that much cash around with them, and Mary would not have given away her very last penny. The girl would want enough to take her away from the convent if she were forced to it. Or, maybe, when she'd recovered, home again — if the fancy took her. Although she was glad to be solvent for at least a little while, a small niggle of worry gnawed at Sister Joan's conscience.

'Maybe Mary would like some orange juice,' Sister Clare said, as she stirred the porridge the next morning. 'It'd be good for her and it doesn't cost an awful lot if you get the supermarket's own brand. You could get some when you go to pay the electricity bill. The post office is just next door.' She pulled the pan from the hotplate, tapped the spoon on the edge and placed it on a saucer.

Joan frowned. 'We mustn't let this money go to our heads, there's a lot to be done. Sister Imelda says that the boiler needs replacing really, so if we call in a professional we can only have it patched up again.' Sister Clare looked so disappointed that she relented and said, 'Oh, all right, I'll get the orange juice. I hope Mary will be kind enough to lend us the car again.'

'She gave you a great deal of money.' Sister Madeline frowned as she pulled a chair up to the table. 'We must be careful. She's very young to have such funds at her disposal.'

'Do you think she's robbed a bank?' Sister Emma's eyes were wide with excitement.

'Doubt it,' said Sister Imelda. 'Not in the heels she was wearing on the way here. Couldn't make a very quick gettaway in those.'

'Oh,' said Emma, with a sigh that sounded like disappointment. 'I suppose not.'

'Her face seems familiar,' said Madeline, 'I can't place it but it's as if I've seen it somewhere — just can't remember. I think maybe she's recognizable. That's why she's scared to go far.'

'Sister,' Joan addressed Madeline. 'I have to ask you to be a little less confrontational in your attitude to Mary. She's only been here a few days — there's plenty of time for her to come to us with her problems. The police are no longer involved, the boyfriend has been found. She is of age and we are not breaking the law by giving her shelter. She's phoned home and her parents know

150

she's safe. We can only wait patiently now — and see what happens.'

Madeline inclined her head in acceptance of her superior's request, but she said, 'With all respect, Mother, it was Mary, you remember, who told us that the boyfriend had been found and the search called off. Can we believe that's all there is to it? That she just doesn't want to see him again? She still doesn't want to venture even as far as our little beach. This boyfriend — maybe he's the one she's running from.' She paused. 'He may be a dangerous thug — or something.'

'Oh! Golly!' gasped Sister Emma.

Sister Joan hated to reprimand any of her nuns, but Madeline — although Joan realized that she only wanted to protect her sisters — had gone too far and Emma was frightened.

'Sister!' She rose from her place at table and moved to the chair beside Madeline to speak quietly to her. She knew that she ought to have taken Madeline to her study to talk to her in private, but the moment was now, and not to be wasted. 'I know you mean to be sensible about this but I fear that your imagination is running away with you. There is no harm in Mary — I believe that implicitly. You must rely on my judgement. This girl has crossed our path and it is our duty to do our best for her. No matter what her problem is, or who she is, she deserves the tender loving care that our Rule demands.' She suddenly realized the meaning of TLC.

'I apologize, Mother — but life — it can be so disappointing sometimes. There are bad people in the world — I don't want any of us to be hurt.' Sister Madeline's eyes suddenly filled with tears.

'I know that, my dear.' She put a comforting hand on Madeline's shoulder. 'You, of all of us, know more about the modern world. You were a part of it for a long time before you came to us. But we must all endeavour to trust. Life is not without some risks that have to be taken and causes for which it's worth facing a little danger. After all, if anything bad happens, PC Bradley is only a phone call away. Mary will confide in us soon and I'm sure that nothing can be too difficult to be sorted out in the Lord's good time.' She smiled at them all. 'Now, eat your breakfast before it gets cold, Sisters.'

Clare began to ladle out the porridge into bowls.

Joan hadn't heard the kitchen door open. Suddenly, Mary's voice said, 'I felt like I could do with a cup of tea — am I too early? I couldn't sleep, but I don't feel so washed out this morning.'

They turned to face her. She stood in the doorway smiling at them. It was obvious that she had heard nothing of their conversation. Everyone gasped in astonishment. Mary had cut off her long blonde hair. It was cropped close to her head and clung around her face in jagged ends. Joan hardly recognized her — it changed her appearance completely. She looked like a small elf.

Coming into the room she grinned and said, 'Not bad is it? Considering I cut it with my nail scissors — it took ages! Bit of a nuisance, all that hanging down my back — more comfy now.'

'But you looked like a film star with all that hair,' mourned Sister Emma. 'Now you look — sort of ordinary.' She clapped a hand to her mouth. 'Oh! I didn't mean to be unkind.'

'Oh, but ordinary is just what I want to be,' smiled Mary. 'Just plain ordinary.' She held up her hands: the nails were cut short and bare of polish. 'By the way, I'm driving to the shops this morning. Can I borrow your wellies, Sister Amy — I'll give them back when I've bought myself some trainers, and I'm pretty desperate for soap,

153

shampoo and all that sort of stuff. Anyone else like to come?' She sat down at the table.

The girl's new-found confidence overwhelmed them — but, thought Joan, was her attitude genuine or was it an act to cover some inner desperation.

No one spoke until Sister Clare said, 'Would you like some toast, Mary?'

The girl blanched. 'No — no thanks. I think I'll skip breakfast if you don't mind. I-I don't feel like eating, just tea please.'

Oh, Mary Winter! thought Joan — whoever knows who you really are would be hard pressed to recognize you now and you look thinner and more pale than ever. Maybe a visit from Doctor Stewart wouldn't be such a bad idea after all. The girl had reduced the conversation in the kitchen to complete silence. The change in her appearance was amazing.

'There's a nice little dress shop at the top of the High Street,' Mary said. 'I think I'll get myself a warm sweater and an anorak.'

Sister Clare, her hand shaking slightly, poured a mug of tea for her and Mary took a sip. 'Next door to the chemist I think,' Mary added.

Joan was startled. They had never described the town to Mary and yet she knew where the boutique was — and the pharmacy. She leaned across the table and touched the girl's hand lightly.

'Have you been there before Mary — to our town?'

Mary was silent for a while then, looking directly into Joan's eyes she said, 'Yes, I've been there before. Now — does anyone want to come with me this morning?'

CHAPTER THIRTEEN

Mary's seemingly new attitude of bravado had rendered the nuns dumbfounded and her confession about having been to their town before had left Sister Joan shocked. Far from being a wanderer — a lost soul seeking peace and quiet in their care, she now appeared to be full of confidence and with a knowledge of where the boutique and the pharmacy were. Her readiness to walk around the town with no fear of being seen came as a complete surprise. Of course, cutting off all her lovely hair would have a lot to do with it, thought Joan, plus the shortening of her fingernails and the removal of the over-bright nail polish. The borrowing of Sister Amy's wellies would no doubt add to the disguise and until Mary bought one of her own, Sister Imelda's big purple anorak would finish the job.

The nuns were all as still as a tableau, just staring at Mary who, appearing quite unconcerned, was sipping the hot tea that Sister Clare had given her. Joan knew that she must be the first to speak.

'You didn't tell us that you'd been here before, Mary?'

'Well — I haven't been exactly — right here,' Mary said, her air of confidence suddenly deflating a little. 'It's just that I-I've been to the town before. Besides, you never asked me.'

'It was hardly the first thing on my agenda,' Joan said. 'When I found you in the lane during the storm and pouring rain and brought you home, I assumed you were lost!'

'Oh, I was lost all right. I was heading for Compton Bay — through the town and along the coast road. When I saw I was running out of fuel I just turned off the road — sort of anywhere — and it just happened to be here and although it seems silly now — I'd completely lost my bearings. It's not like me to let the petrol get so low. I should have topped it up. I was in a bit of a state you know.'

'I'll say you were!' said Joan. 'If I hadn't found you, your situation would have been pretty serious to say the least.'

'Jolly dire, I should say,' murmured Sister Imelda.

'So you had no idea that there was a convent here?' asked Joan.

'No!' answered Mary. 'No idea at all.'

'When were you last in the town then?'

Mary put down her mug of tea. Her small face grew pink and she clasped her hands together and lowered her eyes as if she was loath to tell them. Joan felt that the girl had probably said more than she had intended. The new hair cut and complete change of image had not given her the confidence she had obviously expected. Then she rested her elbows on the table and cupped her chin in her hands.

'I — we used to come here often — Mum, Dad and me — when I was little. To that small bay along the coast road. We used to come for our summer holidays.' She picked up her mug again and took a sip of tea. Joan and the sisters waited, not daring to invade the silence for fear of losing the moment.

'They were such happy times. When I open my window upstairs and hear the sea I can remember so much.' Her eyes moistened. 'Sandcastles, ice cream, the seagulls, and Dad eating cockles in vinegar from those little white saucer things.' She sighed and looked at Sister Joan with eyes that seemed twice as large now under the elfin haircut that she had managed to contrive with her nail scissors. 'Then there was the summer that Mum entered me for the talent contest on the pier. She was a bit pushy, but she loved me very much and always wanted the best for me. I didn't appreciate all the things she did for me at the time. I was fourteen and thought I was the cat's whiskers and could conquer the world all by myself.' She smiled sadly. 'I won the contest — but things were never the same again. I-I just had to come back here again to — remember. I needed to remember how things used to be.'

Joan put her hand over the girl's fingers. 'What do you mean, dear?' she said gently.

Mary withdrew her hand swiftly. 'I don't want to talk about it anymore!'

The atmosphere in the warm kitchen had changed suddenly and Joan felt that the moment was lost.

'But Mary!' Madeline stirred her tea. 'What you've told us seems such a nice memory — can't you tell us more? What happened after you won the contest? What could have changed so much?'

Mary fidgeted uncomfortably on her chair. 'I can't tell you — not yet.'

Sister Clare, moving amongst them topping up the tea mugs, put the teapot down on the table between Sister Joan and Mary and rested her hand affectionately on the girl's shoulder. 'Sure, now — we're all your friends here,' she said softly. 'We're dying to know what happened to you.' She smiled. 'It all sounds like the beginning of a fine adventure to me.'

Suddenly, Mary jumped up, sending the brown teapot crashing to the floor.

'Oh Lord — the teapot!' Sister Clare stepped back as broken pottery and hot tea splattered across the floor.

'I told you — I don't want to talk about it any more!' Mary shouted. 'I shouldn't have said even that much. Oh, gosh! Look what I've done! I shouldn't have been so rude — you're so kind to me and I'm nothing but trouble to you. All I wanted to do was to be where I was happy once. To try to find that little bed and breakfast place again and get back the peace I had — once, a long time ago! Oh! Look at this mess — I must clean it up.'

'Mary.' Joan rose to her feet and put her hand on the girl's arm. 'We don't mean to pry, but how can we help you if you don't tell us the whole story. As things are, all we seem to do is either frighten you or make you cross. First, you want to hide and then you're quite eager to go to town in the very car that you insisted we conceal in the barn.'

'I've cut off my hair — no one will recognize me!'

Madeline spread marmalade on her toast. 'So!' she said quietly. 'You're recognizable, are you?'

Mary turned to Joan. 'There she goes again, Sister! Always picking on me! Get her off my back!'

'A bit of respect wouldn't go amiss,' Imelda said quietly. 'Madeline — like the rest of us — only wants to help!'

'I'm sorry.' Mary dashed away a tear. 'I'll tell you soon but — not now. I'm not ready — really I'm not.'

Sister Clare went to the sink to get the floor cloth from the cupboard underneath.

'Here — I'll clean up this mess.' Mary stepped forward, took the floor cloth and began to mop up the tea leaves. 'Have you got a dustpan for the bits?' she asked contritely.

Mary's activity made the conversation impossible to continue. Joan sighed and moved her chair to let the girl sweep up the shards of brown teapot. The moment was lost. Mary would say no more for the time being.

'Does anyone want to go to town with me this morning, then?' Mary asked quietly when the floor was clean again. 'I'm going

161

about nine-thirty.'

Her wide eyes and air of innocent contrition went to Joan's heart. 'I'll go with you if I may,' she said. 'I have to pay the electricity bill and I need some stamps.'

'Me, too, please,' said Imelda. 'I can pick up Doctor Stewart's strimmer. He needs a repair job done.'

'OK — no bother, see you later then. Thanks for the tea and sorry about all the — oh, you know what.' Mary left the kitchen quickly and went upstairs to her room. Joan heard the door of the guest-room bang shut. A sound to which she was not eager to become accustomed.

'That child exhausts me!' Clare said, 'and the day's only just begun!'

Joan frowned. 'I think she's very scared and very desperate, despite the new image she's created for herself. I feel that there's something important she's wanting to tell us and she doesn't quite know how. I have a feeling that it won't be long before she tells us what all this is about and why she's so keen to be anonymous. Be patient, Sisters.' Joan managed a confident smile.

'And while we're being patient, Mother,' — Sister Clare sighed — 'do you think you could see your way clear to buying us a new teapot while you're in the town? For I don't think we can survive all this excitement without one!'

Sister Imelda sighed. 'First the little radio then the jolly teapot — what next I ask myself?'

Sister Madeline, who had been unusually quiet, said, 'When Mary came down for her tea I don't think she had any intention of telling us about her childhood. Mark my words — there cetainly will be more to come.'

Joan patted Madeline's hand. 'I have a feeling that you're absolutely right Sister.'

Imelda spread low-fat margarine on a thick slice of toast and said, 'She usually is, Mother — she usually is!'

Joan felt that the girl had confided more than ever before, but, she thought, I don't think it's just your identity you want to conceal, Mary Winter. I have a feeling that there's a whole lot more you're hiding from us.

CHAPTER FOURTEEN

The morning mail had been exciting and productive. There was a letter from the local paper saying that they'd be very interested in an article each week about gardening by Sisters Amy and Louise and asked for a sample of one thousand words — double spacing — as soon as possible. Joan was glad now that she'd bucked up courage to write to them about her talented sisters. The money offered would be a great help. The little portable typewriter that had been retired to the cupboard behind her desk could now be brought out and given a good overhaul. Imelda could do that. The next thing to find out was who amongst them could type, for Amy and Louise certainly couldn't. Anyway, if push came to shove she could manage with four fingers, it would only be copy-typing. The two nuns, who were a fount of green-fingered knowledge, would be thrilled with the task of handwriting all the necessary information. She placed the letter in the drawer where she had placed the think tank papers, closed it and sighed contentedly — it was a start anyway and a little closer to funding a watertight roof. She would tell the sisters the good news at lunchtime. Getting up from her chair she made her way to the door, went through and into the hall to put on her coat and gloves ready to go with Mary.

Sister Imelda was there already, in her formal grey coat, pulling on her woollen gloves. 'We'll need the scarves pretty soon, Mother — there's a real bite in the air today.'

Sister Amy had left her wellies on the front doorstep ready to be borrowed and at exactly nine-thirty Mary was there, slipping her grey-socked feet into them. She pulled Imelda's old purple anorak closer about her neck. 'Getting cold, isn't it?' she shivered.

Joan, waiting just by the front door smiled and said, 'It's nearly Christmas, you know, only just over a month to go.'

'Christmas — oh, yes.'

Joan noted that Mary's voice was a little wistfull. Yes, my girl, she thought, you can't run away from everything. There are always anniversaries of something or other to bring

the world back into your focus again —
whether it be for joy or sadness.

'You wait here, Sisters — I'll get the car
out and pick you up. Is the barn locked?'

'No, I've unlocked it already,' said Imelda.

Mary stalked off across the gravel drive in
the keen east wind and the unfamiliar wellingtons, with the anorak flapping around
her small body. She came back at the wheel
of the Porsche, stopped the engine, got out
and opened the doors for her passengers.

'Hop in out of the cold, Sisters, you'll
soon warm up, I've got the heater on.' She
had also put a CD in the player. It wasn't
the loud and brash one that Sister Imelda
had found.

'You'll like this one, I think.' She smiled at
Joan. 'Gregorian Chant — you'll probably
find this hard to believe but — I play it a
lot. It sort of calms your mind.' She put the
car into gear and drove carefully out of the
drive and into the lane. 'This motor's filthy
— needs to go through the car wash.'

'That would attract attention don't you
think? I should clean it in the barn if I were
you, Mary — it'll cost nothing.' Joan smiled.
The girl was silent.

She was surprised to note that Mary
didn't drive as fast as Sister Imelda, but
maybe that was because she was more

familiar with the feel of a powerful car and was not so excited by it.

'How did you come by this CD?' Joan was curious.

'It was Allan, my boyfriend — he bought it for me, when I was feeling a bit manic. It made me realize that there are good things in the world, if you take the time to look and to listen. Blooming good at the harmony aren't they? You see, I know a fair bit about music. They're these Italian monks — they've been singing like that for years and years. Like — hundreds! You'd think someone would have cottoned on to it ages ago. It's great after a party when you want to chill out. Or if you just want to — to forget something for a while. Anyway, it's just cool.' She smiled and joined in at what must have been a familiar piece and although her Latin had obviously been learned by listening to the recording time and time again, and her pronunciation a little shaky, her voice was sweet and a complete contrast to the male choir, yet it blended perfectly.

'That was lovely, Mary,' Joan said when the piece was finished. 'Where in heaven's name did you learn to sing like that?'

At the top of the lane just before the main road Mary stopped the car and, turning to

167

Joan, she said, 'Oh, I've done a bit of singing — here and there.' Putting the car into gear she turned onto the highway.

They drove in silence — even Sister Imelda remained quiet — as they listened to the Italian monks. Oh, to achieve such harmony, thought Joan wistfully, thinking of their early mornings in the chapel.

'If you stop at Len Harvey's garage, Mary, we can walk into the town from there. It'll only take a couple of minutes. Then Sister Imelda can take the car and pick up Doctor Stewart's strimmer — would that be OK?' Joan asked, as they approached the town.

'Sure,' replied Mary. 'Good idea, we won't have to park the car in the middle of the town. We can all meet up again back at the garage when we've done our bits of shopping. You won't mind driving again will you, Sister?' she grinned at Imelda.

'I should jolly well think not!' Imelda laughed. 'It'll be a privilege. By the way, Len's garage is just round the next bend.'

'Well, don't break the sound barrier when you're in the driver's seat.' Mary changed gear and turned left into the top of the town, then left again onto Len Harvey's forecourt, bringing the Porsche to a smooth halt beside a small green car that Len was polishing. He straightened up when he saw them.

'My word — now isn't that a good advertisement for my old garage!' he grinned. 'Travelling in the fast lane again, Sisters?' He came forward to Joan's side of the car to let her out.

She glanced at Mary and noticed the tension in the girl's face. Of course, she would not have expected to be confronted by Len. Mary opened her door and, moving around to let Sister Imelda out, she pressed the car keys into her hand.

'There you are, Sister,' she said. 'Drive carefully. See you both later back here and, by the way, *I'm* buying the teapot.' Pulling the purple anorak closer around her neck she scuttled off toward the shops without another word.

'That your visitor?' Len asked, eyeing the girl with curiosity.

'Yes,' Joan said. 'She — she's rather shy.'

Len sighed, 'Rare that, nowadays. Nice to see.'

'Indeed it is,' Joan replied. She realized, however, that Mary's new-found confidence had been tried and was found wanting. The girl was scared. 'We mustn't keep you, Len, you'll want to be getting on with your polishing,' said Joan. 'Sister is off to Doctor

Stewart's to pick up a strimmer for repair. Will it be OK for us to meet up back here again when we've done our shopping? It'll save having to park in the middle of the town. Sister Imelda will take it around the back if you like.'

Len smiled broadly. 'Oh no, Sister — you park that there Porsche right here in front of me workshop. I haven't had something so good for business on me forecourt for a long while. You feel free to wait for as long as you like.' He waved as Sister Imelda pulled away from the garage and continued his polishing as Joan walked down to the High Street shops in the wake of Mary, who had long since gone from sight.

It was a joy to be able to pay the electricity bill so promptly. Was it just her imagination or did the girl behind the counter look surprised to see that it wasn't the red one? I'm getting too sensitive, thought Joan. She came out of the post office and went into the supermarket next door to get the promised orange juice for Sister Clare to give Mary for breakfast the next morning. Maybe after that the girl could be persuaded to eat a little. She hadn't touched the bar of chocolate that she'd bought on the previous shopping trip. No doubt she was dieting.

That was a big worry. Mary had the appetite of a bird — the girl needed strength.

She made her way back to the garage. Imelda was already back with the car and when she arrived it was to find Mary putting a large box into the boot along with a plastic bag from the pharmacy.

'Would you mind waiting in the car for a while?' she asked. 'I've just got a bit more to do before we go back.'

'Not at all, dear,' said Joan. 'Imelda and I shall enjoy watching the world go by.'

Imelda leaned over and opened the door on the passenger side and Joan eased herself into the low seat. 'I've something to tell you all at lunchtime,' she said, as they watched Mary walking off down to the shops again.

'About Mary?' Imelda asked.

'No — but it's something nice.' Telling the nuns about the letter inviting Amy and Louise to write the gardening article would be a great pleasure. She pressed the button that opened the window of the car a little.

'Has something positive happened for a change then?' asked Imelda. 'I've been doing an awful lot of praying about our situation.'

Joan smiled, 'Yes, Sister, it is a positive thing.'

'Gracious — I can hardly bear to wait,'

Imelda said — but she would never have asked to be told before her sisters.

Joan took a deep breath and settled back into the comfortable seat.

'Planning your next heist, Sisters?' Len Harvey tapped on the window. 'You'd never have made a quick getaway in that old Ford of yours!'

Joan jumped and laughed, 'Oh, Len — you did give me a fright.' She lowered the window so that she could talk to him.

'Sister Imelda at the wheel again I see,' he grinned.

'Our — our visitor wanted some extra shopping so we're waiting for a while.'

'Oh, that's OK — long as you like. Want some tea?' he smiled.

'That's very nice of you, Len, but no thank you. Mary shouldn't be too long. Then we must get home.'

'So, Mary, is it? The lad told me about your guest — quite taken with her, he is. Quiet little thing, ain't she? Funny hair-do she's got — pardon me saying. Don't look no more than a child. Not the sort that usually drives around in a motor like this.' He patted the roof of the car.

'Yes, she's very quiet. How are you Len and how is your wife?' Joan changed the subject.

172

'Oh, I'm fine, thanks, but me Missus has got the flu and the lad is very upset at the moment.'

'Oh, Len, what's happened?'

'You know that concert he and his mate were saving up to go and see?'

'Yes.'

'Well, it's been cancelled. Star's gone missing or something. It's that Gucci Foot girl with the long blonde hair and the 'orrible shoes. Heaven only knows — pardon the expression, Reverend — how she walks in 'em. Let alone do three hours on the stage dancing about and singing the while. You'd think the world had come to an end for the lad and his mate Fred. I said to 'em, it'll get put on again, they'll find her, you'll just have to wait a bit longer that's all. That wasn't no comfort to 'em though. You know youngsters, want everything immediate they do. I've never seen the lad look so miserable and it's the devil's own job — pardon me again, Reverend — to get him to do a stroke of work in the garage.'

'Oh, poor boys, these things mean so much at their age,' Joan said.

'Yeah, really cut up about it he is. He's got a poster of her up in his room. Never seen a lass so pale and thin. Looks like she lives on lettuce and lemon juice. It's a hard life for these young pop stars, stress must be bloomin' unbearable — no wonder she's done a runner. So I says to him I says' — Len continued — 'you'd better have the rest of the day off if you're not going to do anything around here. Have all your miseries about it and come back fresh in the morning. So he's gone home and I've got two gaskets to do on me own before teatime,' he sighed.

'Len, I'm so sorry.' Joan patted the grimy fingers that were curled over the edge of the car window. 'You're such an understanding man.'

'Yes, jolly kind,' added Imelda. 'I'd help with the gaskets only I don't have the time or the overalls.'

Len Harvey blushed. 'Oh, don't give it no mind. I shouldn't worry you both with my troubles. By the way, I've got a buyer for your old Ford. Bloke wants it for spares, so he does. He'll give you a good price. You'd get less than nothing for scrap. In fact, it would cost you a tidy penny to have it towed away. You have a think about it — you and Sister Spanner — and give me a call if you're interested, eh? Must be off. I'm as busy as you are' — he grinned at Sister Imelda — 'ain't no rest for us mechanics.' He smiled, touched the peak of his greasy cap and began to walk away. Suddenly, he turned back and said, 'Funny thing, now — just the other day a chap came in here and asked me if I'd seen a car like this one. Only thing was, the girl what he described to be driving it had long hair and was dressed posh. I said I'd not seen anyone like that. Your visitor don't look likely, do she? Must be more than a few youngsters with rich daddies driving around in cars like this. In my young day a pushbike was luxury!' He laughed and went into his workshop carrying a paper bag with Compton Bakeries printed on the front, that probably contained his lunch.

Something began to stir in Joan's imagination. Mary's singing in the car on the way to town — winning a talent contest when she was fourteen — Len Harvey's lad being disappointed — those awful sandals — the thin pale girl — the missing person announcement on their little radio before it was smashed. Someone asking questions. The pieces whirled together in her mind like an unfinished jigsaw puzzle. She caught Imelda's eye. Her sister said nothing but the look in her eyes said, are you thinking what I'm thinking?

Imelda found the radio and without a word she switched it on and began listening to a quiz show. Joan watched the passers-by, conscious that Imelda was giving her superior uninterrupted time to think. Glancing over the road she noticed that the office of their local newspaper, the *Compton Gazette,* was directly opposite. An idea occured to her. Opening her door she said, 'Only be a moment, Sister — back soon.'

Imelda smiled and nodded, now totaly engrossed in the quiz.

Making her way carefully across the busy street she opened the door of the *Gazette* office and stepped inside. There was a thickly carpeted reception area with comfortable chairs by a large front window and a counter at the far end, behind this was a young lady receptionist. The room smelled of polish and had an air of efficiency about it that almost disconcerted her. Taking a deep breath she approached the reception desk.

'Good morning, Sister — how can I help you?' The girl was friendly and put Joan immediately at her ease.

'Well, I don't know if you can help me but I thought it might be worth a try.' Feeling very guilty she took a deep breath. 'Some years ago, maybe six or seven, there was a talent contest at the town hall. I wonder if you have a record of the winner?'

The girl smiled. 'Oh! The talent contest! Yes, we have one every year you know. We always send a reporter and cameraman to cover it. What year were you interested in?'

'Well, I'm not quite sure. Maybe six years ago, maybe we should start there.'

'Right ho,' said the girl. 'It'll only take a jiff.' She sat down at her computer keyboard and got to work. It seemed like no time at all before she said, 'Here we are. All the details and a photo of the winner — I've done you a print-out.' She handed the copy to Joan. The picture was of a young man of about thirteen holding a violin.

'Oh!' exclaimed Joan. 'It — it isn't quite what I'd expected.'

'Not the one?' the girl asked.

'I'm afraid not.' Joan couldn't help feeling disappointed along with an extra feeling of guilt. Maybe, she thought, I should stop right there. I'm really prying and I don't like the feeling.

'Never mind,' said the girl. 'Let's give it another try — let's try seven years ago.' She was back at the keyboard before Joan could stop her.

'You — you're very kind, thank you,' she managed to say.

'No bother — I love doing research.' The girl tapped busily at her computer.

Joan began to think that she really shouldn't be doing this. It felt rather sneaky now, after what had seemed a sensible idea. Was she betraying Mary? No, she thought, anything I can do to find the truth can only be a good thing as far as Mary is concerned. She glanced out through the window and over the road. Imelda was still in the driving seat laughing silently at whatever was on the radio and Mary was nowhere to be seen. Oh, please hurry, she thought, I don't want Mary to see me coming out of here.

'There we are,' the girl said at last. 'Maybe we're lucky this time.' She handed the printout over the counter to Joan. The photograph was of a young thin teenager with long blonde hair. 'Looks just like an angel, doesn't she,' the girl smiled.

There was no time to read the caption below the picture. Just as she took the paper from the girl, Joan glanced out of the window and saw Mary coming up the High Street towards the car. She took the paper, folded it without looking at it and stuffed it into her pocket. 'Thank you so much,' she said to the suprised girl. 'How much will that cost?'

'Oh, nothing at all, Sister — it was a pleasure. I hope I've helped.'

'Bless you, my dear, you certainly have —

thank you so very much.' She hurried out of the shop, negotiated the busy road and arrived back at the car just before Mary.

'What a huge amount of shopping, Mary — do you really need all that?' she asked breathlessly.

'I certainly do, Sister.' Mary grinned. She opened the bonnet and rammed her shopping in on top of the dismantled strimmer and the other parcels. Closing it, she came round to the driver's side and spoke through the window to Imelda. 'You want to drive home Sister?'

'Oh, yes, please — I'd be delighted,' said Imelda.

'I'll sit in the back with Sister Joan then.' Mary smiled, opened the offside door for Joan then went around to the other side opened the door and squeezed down beside her almost in one movement. 'Wow!' she said. 'That was a marathon shopping spree. The hardware shop had a teapot just the same as the one that I — that got broken at breakfast and I've got two warm jumpers, another pair of jeans, a couple of T-shirts, lots of socks, some trainers and a pair of wellies that really fit, an amazing woolly hat with "I Hate Cold Weather" emboidered on the front and' — she stopped to take a breath and grinned at Joan — 'some extra scanties.'

'Well!' said Joan. 'That seems sensible enough and you'll be pleased to have your anorak all to yourself again, won't you, Imelda?'

'Yes, I shall — old thing's jolly handy,' Imelda laughed.

'Mary, you must have spent an awesome amount of money.' It seemed to Joan that Mary was intending to stay for quite some time.

'I've got enough,' Mary said quietly. Then, changing the subject, she said, 'There's a Frank Sinatra CD in the glovebox, sister. Let's have that one on the way back.'

Imelda found it and put it into the player with what was becoming an air of expertise. 'Here comes Ol' Blue Eyes,' she laughed.

Joan smiled. 'As a matter of fact,' she said, 'I used to be quite a fan of his, once upon a time.'

Mary glanced at Joan in wonder. 'Wicked!' she said. 'Cool, wasn't he?'

'Yes Mary, I suppose he was.'

'Er — I quite liked him, too,' said Imelda shyly.

When they were all settled with their seat belts on, Imelda turned the key in the ignition and the Porsche glided like silk off Len Harvey's forecourt and into the road to the sound of Frank Sinatra telling everyone 'Come Fly With Me'.

Joan put her hand into her pocket and felt the folded paper. She was burning with guilty curiosity. This could be at least part of the answer to some of the questions in her mind about Mary, or maybe all of them. At the very least it would reveal her real name. She would leave the paper in her pocket, hang up the coat in the hall cupboard as usual and refer to it later in privacy. The whole business felt exciting — but on the other hand it made her feel more like a criminal than a sleuth. Was she betraying Mary's trust? Maybe she should put the paper into the kitchen stove to burn away and let the situation evolve at Mary's own pace. No, she couldn't do that. She was so near to finding out the truth. The glimpse she had had of the photograph on the printout was unmistakable — it was definitely a young Mary. She had gone beyond the point of no return now. She let go the paper and folded her hands on her lap.

'I saw you coming out of the newspaper office,' Mary said innocently.

Joan's face grew suddenly hot with embarassment. Please, she thought, don't ask what I was doing there — but surely that's exactly what the girl would want to know.

'You wrote to the paper didn't you? Are they going to let the sisters do the gardening article then?'

Joan took a deep breath of relief and answered truthfully. 'Yes, Mary, I do believe they are.'

'Good-oh,' Mary said.

Frank Sinatra sang 'Luck Be a Lady' as Sister Joan's heart beat hard under the silver crucifix that hung around her neck and he finished his 'Very Good Year' as they pulled up outside the front door of the Stella Maris Convent.

'Home safe and sound,' said Sister Imelda.

Joan felt that it had been one of the longest journeys of her life.

CHAPTER FIFTEEN

Sister Clare held up her hands in amazement as Mary came back and forth from the car to the hall, piling up the carrier bags and finishing with the large box.

'What's in this supermarket bag?' she asked Joan.

'Orange juice — Sister Clare thought you might like it at breakfast.'

'You're a flock of angels you lot, but I told you not to spend money on posh stuff for me.'

'Oh, it isn't that posh, but it's good stuff.' Joan laughed. 'It's the supermarket's own brand, but it does mean that you can have a lot more for your money. As for the rest, you'll have to take potluck with us.'

Mary picked up the box. 'Can you bring the green bag from the chemist's please, Sister.' She grinned at Joan. 'I've got some bits and pieces in it for you all. Oh, and the teapot's in the blue bag.' Once in the kitchen Mary put the box on the table. 'Go on,' she said to Sister Imelda, 'you open it!'

Imelda thrust a powerful thumb nail along the parcel tape that sealed the box and pulled back the flaps of the lid. 'Lor-o-lumme what's this?' she said, withdrawing a bright red object with a handle on the top. 'It's a jolly radio!' she exclaimed.

Mary clapped her hands with delight. 'Do you like it — do you really like it? It goes on batteries or mains and you can get all the stations in the world! Look — here's the aerial.' She lifted up a telescopic device on the top and pulled it up to its full height. 'Switch it on, Sister — go on!'

Sister Imelda turned on the radio and got Spain then France and finally the BBC. 'It's wonderful, Mary. Now I don't have to fiddle around with the DIY crystal set my brother gave me for Christmas. Couldn't get the jolly thing to work anyway!' She dashed away a tear. 'That's so nice of you, Mary.'

'It's only fair — after all, I did put paid to your old one, didn't I?'

'You certainly did, child, but now you've redeemed yourself and you deserve a nice cup of tea. The new teapot is perfect.' Sister Clare was blushing with pleasure and clattered cups and plates to the sounds of Classic FM.

Mary sat down at the table. Her face was pink with delight like a child at a birthday party. 'That's not all — later on, something else is coming. I couldn't bring it in the car, but it's a big surprise and I can't wait to see your faces.'

Joan caught her breath. 'Mary, you shouldn't do this, it's — it's far too much.' She thought of the envelope of cash that Mary had already given her for her keep.

'Oh dear, oh lumme — what now?' breathed Imelda.

'Well! Right now there's this.' Mary reached into the green carrier bag and brought out a large jar. 'This is for you, Sister.' She handed it to Imelda.

'What's this, then?' Imelda looked at the label. 'Well, it's jolly barrier cream!'

Mary grinned. 'It's for your hands so they won't get sore when you clean off the grease.'

'Oh, Mary.'

'It's supposed to be very good — the chemist said so,' said Mary eagerly.

'Oh, my dear child — I know it is. Thank you so much.' Imelda patted Mary's cheek.

'And this is for you, Sister Clare.' She handed Clare a brightly labelled bottle. 'It's hand cream — because you have your hands in water so much, what with all the cooking

185

and that.'

'Dear child, you shouldn't do this.'

'Yes, I should — I was a perfect stranger — well maybe not that perfect — but you took me in and cared for me. It's the only way I know how to say thank you.'

'Mary, all you had to do was to say just that.' Joan smiled at her. 'But, my dear, we are most grateful for your thoughtful gifts.'

There was a little something for everyone. Not extravagant, Joan was pleased to note, but all useful and special to the person for whom they were intended, although every-thing could be used by all. Joan noted that Mary had not been unobservant and had obviously seen that they shared everything. This was not a girl who had ever been purposely unkind, surely.

'And — what is this special thing that we're all to wait patiently for?' Joan asked.

Mary put her elbows on the table and cupped her chin in her hands. 'Not telling — big surprise,' she grinned.

Sister Madeline looked at the packet of herbal teas that Mary had selected for her. 'I shall make good use of these, thank you, Mary,' she said. Then looking quizzically at her, 'Life is getting more and more interest-ing each day you are with us, child. You've certainly been buying — a lot of things.'

Joan was startled. It was the way Madeline had said it. Has Mary been buying us, she thought? Surely not, the girl just has a generous nature and showering them with gifts was the only way she could show her feelings, wasn't it? Oh, Madeline, why do you make me doubt?

'I think that'll be enough excitement for now, don't you agree, Mother?' asked Clare. 'Lunch is almost on the table if we can make room for it.'

'Oh good, I'm really hungry,' said Mary.

Sister Madeline smiled. 'Missing breakfast is no way to look after your figure, if that's what you think you're doing child. You should always make a good start to the day.'

'I-I don't like breakfast.' Mary glowered.

'Well,' said Imelda, pulling a chair up to the table, 'I like everything!'

Joan said grace and smiled as they all tucked into Clare's soup and home-made bread rolls and relished the thought of telling them the news she'd had from the local newspaper this morning. Was it only this morning? It seemed an age ago. She thought of the folded paper in her coat pocket, now safely shut in the hall cupboard. How different things would become when she read it at last.

187

■ ■ ■ ■

They had been so deep in conversation that none of them had noticed the sound of a motor in the driveway, so the sound of the doorbell came as a complete surprise.

'Oh good! It's here already!' Mary said and, jumping up from her chair, went with Sister Clare into the hall.

Joan and the other nuns followed close behind and watched as Clare opened the front door. A man stood on the doorstep muffled up against the cold. 'Is this the Stella Maris Convent?' he asked.

'Sure and don't I look the very image of a nun?' smiled Clare. 'Indeed it is.'

'I'll bring it in then and you can tell me where you want it set up.' He returned to a white van and opened the back doors.

'Oh my, what's the jolly girl gone and done now!' Imelda groaned.

Mary could hardly contain her delight and indeed made no effort to do so. She shifted restlessly from foot to foot and clapped her hands. 'You wait! Oh you just wait and see.'

The man managed to lift a heavy box onto a trolley which he had removed from the back of the van and began to pull it backwards up the front steps one at a time and into the hall.

'Where do you want it?' he puffed, looking ruefully at the long flight of stairs leading to the upper rooms. 'It's a bit heavy and I don't want to be lumbering it all the way up them stairs if you don't mind.'

'We — we don't know what it is,' said Joan. 'It's meant to be a surprise.' She turned to Mary. 'Where do you think your surprise would be most comfortable?'

'Oh, in your living-room, where you go to read and do your sewing, that'll be the best place for it.'

'Lead on then, Macduff,' said the man as he grabbed the handles of the trolley once more.

There was a gasp from all of them as the contents of the box revealed a television set.

'It's just what you need, isn't it?' Mary's face was glowing with happiness. 'Now you'll never have a dull evening ever again.'

Sister Flora patted her arm. 'We never have dull evenings, dear, but it's a beautiful gift and I'm sure we're all delighted.' She nudged Joan gently. 'Aren't we, Sister?'

Joan was almost speechless as were the other nuns. I mustn't hurt Mary's feelings, she thought, but this is far too generous a gift. It was hard to be enthusiastic, there were too many questions reeling around in

189

her mind. She tried to work out how many roof tiles could be bought for the cost of the television, but had no idea what its price would have been anyway. Mary was being too generous, too showy.

She took the girl's hand. 'Mary — it's, it's a very large gift dear and — and now we have to get a licence for it. I-I think, well, we can't really afford it you know.'

'Oh!' said Mary gleefully. 'I've already thought of that. I went to the post office and got you a licence too. It's all ready to go — cool, isn't it?'

Imelda found her voice at last and said, 'Lumme, it's a big 'n. Room'll be like a jolly cinema!'

'It's only a twenty-one inch,' said the television man. 'Just the right size for a room like this. You chose well, miss,' he said to Mary, 'I'll tune it in for you. It'll be ready to roll in no time at all. Look, here's the remote control.'

'Well, I never!' said Sister Imelda. 'I thought that was some sort of mobile phone that came free with the set!'

Mary grinned, her cropped hair and bright cheeks made her look more like an elf than ever. 'I just knew you'd like it — magic, isn't it?'

The weather forecast suddenly appeared

on the screen. 'Oh my, it's a coloured picture!' gasped Sister Flora.

The man looked incredulous. 'Good grief, you have been out of touch,' he said and, glancing at the screen, 'look at that — storm warning — east coast. One of them roarers we get this time of the year around here. Batten down the hatches, Sisters, although sometimes these storms don't always come to much.' He waited until the forecast was over. 'Well, better be on my way. Any problems with the telly, just give us a ring.' He handed Joan a card. 'Always ready to oblige.'

None of them could drag her eyes away from the screen except Sister Clare, who showed him politely to the door and bade him good day.

It was nearly bedtime but Joan was loath to drag them away from the game show on the new television. Sister Flora had got every question right and would have won a million pounds if she'd been in the chair instead of the contestant.

'Well done, Flora.' Imelda clapped her hands. 'I'd never have got the one about the doughnuts!'

'Oh, I knew that one,' Clare said, 'but I'm not so hot on the mathematics.'

Joan drew Mary aside. 'My dear,' she whispered. 'I want to thank you for your kindness to us but something worries me very much and I feel we have to talk about it.'

Mary's face grew serious and Joan could see that she was already drawing up barriers around herself. Don't ask me anything — don't get too near me — I don't want to answer any questions, said the defensive expression on the little face.

Joan took her hand and spoke quietly to her. The nuns were engrossed in the television and paid no attention to them. 'Mary, it's the money. Where in the world did you get so much money? How does someone of your tender years have access to so much? Even the sisters have commented quietly to me. This is a simple country seaside town; spending like this will be noticed, people will talk. You expressed a wish to be anonymous. Have you changed your mind now?'

'I haven't spent that much,' Mary said.

'Maybe not by your standards, Mary, but all these things — it's a lot to us.'

'I didn't pay cash for the telly. I used my plastic,' Mary grinned.

'Mary, I may be a nun and slightly removed from worldly things but can't you be traced if you've paid by credit card?'

It was a shock to Joan when Mary reddened and said, 'Damn! I don't know! Maybe! I was so excited about buying it for you — I never thought of that. Of course I don't want to be found!'

A peal of laughter rose up from the direction of the television set. The nuns were watching a situation comedy and hadn't noticed Mary's outburst.

The girl looked directly into Joan's eyes. 'If anyone comes asking — you haven't seen me — right?'

'I'm not going to lie for you, Mary — it would do you no good at all and certainly no good to us.'

'You said you'd help me. The money is legitimate — I earned it. It's mine, I told you before, there's nothing criminal about what I'm doing. I haven't stolen it or anything.'

'Then, Mary, tell me everything, here — now. You can trust me, my very vocation is to help.' Tell me, Mary, Joan thought, then there will be no need for me to play detective and sneak off to read that paper I got from the *Gazette* office.

'No!' Mary said forcefully. 'I won't — and you can't make me. If I did you — you'd hate me — all of you would hate me and you'd turn me out! I'll sort my problems out for myself. Then — I'll tell you.'

'Mary! There couldn't be anything that would make us turn you out!'

The girl was silent for a while. 'Oh yes, there is,' she said quietly.

Joan suddenly noticed that the wind had picked up and was whistling through the chimneys. It was a portent of heavy weather. The rain pattered on the window. She shivered and hoped that the old tiles would hold onto the roof just for a little while longer. She felt weary and longed for her bed. 'Mary, if you won't tell me then I can't make you. We'll leave this conversation for the time being. Maybe you'll feel less tired in the morning, then you can come to my study and we'll talk again.'

Mary gave her a wan smile. 'No, I won't feel any different, sister — I don't want to talk about anything — not yet.'

Joan sighed and turned to the nuns who were loath to be drawn away from the television. 'Bedtime, Sisters, it's time for chapel then sleep. I'm sure that despite the weather every one of us will have a good night's rest after all the excitement today — thank you, Mary, for bringing about such a change in our lives.'

Mary gave a wry grin and said, 'That's cool, Sister!'

194

Just as she spoke the wind howled louder and Joan heard a crash outside. The television went off and so did the lights.

'Oh lumme — a power cut,' said Imelda.

The light from the fireplace gave enough illumination for Joan to find a torch in the drawer of the sideboard. 'I'll get candles from the chapel,' she said. 'There are plenty in the box by the altar.'

Unusually for the time of year a bolt of lightning lit up the room, followed directly by a clap of thunder.

'Bit spooky that — I don't like it.' Mary moved closer to Imelda.

Joan smiled secretly. Gone was the feisty young woman of a few moments ago who thought she could manage the world all by herself.

'This lot'll bring some jolly firewood down,' said Imelda. 'That crash sounded just like a tree falling. Probably that old dead oak by the gates, it's been a bit wobbly for ages. There'll be some clearing up in the morning, mark my words! Don't let the thunder worry you, Mary — nothing scary about it — just heaven's electrics.'

As Joan made her way to the chapel to get the candles, she paused by the hall cupboard, opened the door and reached into her coat pocket for the paper. Withdrawing it she unfolded it with difficulty with the torch in one hand and shone the light on the photograph and the text. It took only a few seconds. Folding the paper again she returned it to her pocket, shut the door of the cupboard and continued on to the chapel. Shafts of lightning lit the way briefly from time to time. She found the candles and a box of matches and made her way back to the living-room. It's strange, she thought, how the darkness and the storm make everything seem like another world. The lightning illuminated the dark old paintings of past Superiors hanging on the walls that went almost unnoticed until anniversary days. They were being afforded more light than ever before and somehow were endowed with more humanity than Joan had ever seen in them. She felt an affinity with those past nuns — you had your problems, too, she thought. What would you have done about Mary Winter?

'Oh good, the jolly candles!' Imelda said with relief as Joan entered the living-room. 'Now we have light!'

'Maybe we should check the fuse box,' Joan said, 'to see if the one for the lights has blown.'

Imelda smiled ruefully. 'Just looked out of

the window, Sister. Problem's a bit more serious than that. The old oak tree's fallen down and taken the phone line and power line with it. We're stuck, I'm afraid — at least until daylight. Completely cut off!'

'No, we're not,' said Mary. 'What about my mobile? We can phone someone and get help.'

'Oh Mary! Of course — you dear girl,' said Imelda. 'I'd forgotton your technology. Well done! Hop upstairs and get it then. We'll phone Bill Murray up at the farm shall we, Mother? He's got a generator — that's if he's not using it.' She looked at Joan for approval.

'Yes,' replied Joan. 'That would be a very good idea.'

'Not on my own,' said Mary. 'I'm not going up there in the dark.'

'Have the jolly torch then, child — make haste!' laughed Imelda.

'Not on my own.' Mary was adamant.

Joan put her hand on the girl's arm. 'I'll come with you,' she said gently.

'Thanks, Sister — it's just that I-I don't like the dark very much.'

'Jolly daft that!' Imelda said. 'There's nothing in the dark that wasn't there when the light was on!'

Joan could hear the nuns chattering as she

and Mary made their way up the stairs to the guest room. As they reached the landing Joan turned to Mary and said, 'You don't have to have that talk with me tomorrow after all — if you really don't want to. I'm not going to insist.' After each fork of lightning the darkness seemed to make everything around them extra black and silent as Mary looked at Joan in the light of the torch.

'How come the change of heart?' she asked quietly.

Her eyes seemed huge, the pupils enlarged by the darkness as she looked at Joan with curiosity from under the ragged haircut.

'Because, Mary Winter' — Joan put her hand on the girl's shoulder — 'I know who you really are!'

CHAPTER SIXTEEN

The storm that had been raging directly overhead now began to rumble away in the distance, leaving only the sound of the rain lashing against the windows of the upper landing and an occasional flash of lightning.

Sister Joan and Mary looked at one another in the torchlight, a smile playing around the girl's lips. 'You're joking!' she said. 'You don't mean that!'

'I wouldn't be flippant about something as serious as this, Mary. I do know who you really are.' Another flash of lightning illuminated the scene, and Joan could see that the smile had vanished from Mary's face.

'But what makes you think that I'm not who I say I am? Everyone knows I'm Mary Winter!' the girl's small chin stuck out defiantly.

'I never really believed you when you told me your name — that night when we took you in and I settled you into the little guest room. I had a feeling that you hadn't told me the truth. It didn't seem important at that moment, but then things seemed to add up and fall into some sort of order. When you mentioned that you'd been here some years ago and had won a talent contest in the town I decided to do some detective work. I went to the *Compton Gazette* office and asked the girl in reception to do some research for me. She looked through the files on her computer to see what she could find — and the result was quite positive. I have a photograph and a print-out of the whole report. I do know who you are.'

'That was a sneaky thing to do — but it's all wrong! I am Mary Winter!' The girl's eyes were wide with panic.

'No,' said Joan quietly, 'I'm not wrong — and don't think that prying was an easy thing for me to do — it wasn't! But it was time for the truth.'

'You're trying to trick me!'

'Rebecca Marie Thornton — I have no need to trick you.'

Mary clung onto the the rail at the head of the stairs. Joan thought she was about to faint but she regained her composure.

'So — you do know,' she said quietly.

'Yes, my dear. You're the Beccy-Marie for

whom everyone is looking. The Gucci Foot who has let down so many people who rely on her for their very livelihoods, so many friends and even her own parents, to run off because it appears that she just felt like it. Now you have to tell me exactly why?'

They faced one another at the top of the stairs, the atmosphere becoming colder, not just between the two of them but a chill in the air as the old house cooled down with the failure of the central heating boiler. Joan felt so close to the truth about this girl that she had almost forgotton why they'd gone upstairs in the first place. As Mary opened her mouth to reply there was the sound of movement in the hall below.

'You've been a jolly long time getting that mobile phone. . . .' Sister Imelda's voice rose above the wind and rain bringing Joan back to their present situation.

'Everything OK up there?'

'Yes,' Mary called. 'We're all right — be down in a sec.'

'Right ho — I'll go back to the fire, it's getting jolly cold out here.'

Mary moved closer to Joan and whispered, 'Do the others know? They've been very quiet about it if they do!'

'No — I'm the only one who knows for sure. Sister Imelda, I'm certain, suspects, but she'd never say anything to the others unless I speak first.'

'They — they don't have to know, do they?' Mary moved towards the guest room followed by Joan. She opened the door and they went inside.

'They'll have to be told, Mary, because from now on we'll really be able to help you — protect you if that is your need — and sort out all this mystery.' She handed the torch to the girl and Mary took it and found the holdall. The phone was on top of her belongings in the bag.

'But you won't have to tell anyone else, will you?' she pleaded. 'Not for a little while longer anyway?'

'Your "little while" is wearing a bit thin, Mary,' Joan sighed. 'We can't give your parents any more anxiety. It's time to stop all this nonsense and tell them exactly where you are.'

'I'll give you more money — I've got plenty of cash.' Mary put the mobile phone into the back pocket of her jeans.

'It's not a case of more money, my dear. You and your well-being are more important to us than that. If you're running away from some sort of danger, then we must help you all we can. If you're just trying to escape the rat-race of the pop world, then there's no better place than being with us to get your breathing space.'

'Then — can we get this storm thing over first?' Mary said quietly. 'The Sisters are waiting for us to get back with the mobile.'

Of course, the girl was right, first things first. They'd had no light or power since the old oak tree had fallen across the lane and pulled down all the wires with it. They had the Rayburn stove in the kitchen and plenty of candles, there was a fire in the living-room, but it looked as if it was going to be a long cold night in their bedrooms. She thought of those nuns of old — this was a situation to which they were well accustomed. Without the need of modern standards and technology, living must have been considerably less expensive. Joan shivered in her fully washable, light grey habit. Times change, she thought, and people were faced with new and different challenges in the world of today. She smiled wryly to herself — and Mary Winter was going to be one of theirs. Being chilly was the least of her worries right now.

When Joan and Mary returned to the living-room the nuns were sitting around the fireplace. They looked cosy and the light from the logs played on their faces as they held out their hands to the warmth. There was music playing.

'Good job we've got the radio, Mary.' Sister Imelda beamed. 'Nice concert on Classic FM — very calming.'

Joan went over to the sideboard and picked up a notebook. 'There's Bill Murray's number, Mary — if you press the buttons I'll talk to him.'

'OK.' Mary operated the mobile and held it to her ear. 'No one answering,' she said after a while.

'Oh lumme — how silly!' Imelda thumped her fist into her other hand. 'If our line is down, then he's cut off too — all the lines go from here over to the farm!'

'Has he got a mobile?' Mary asked.

'My dear,' Joan sighed, 'I've no idea.' She straightened. 'Well Sisters, we're not in any immediate danger. We're warm in here, there's plenty of fuel for the stove so we can make tea in the kitchen and we can wear our dressing-gowns in bed tonight. The morning will come and everything will become more positive in the light.'

'We could phone Constable Bradley on the mobile,' suggested Sister Madeline, 'but there may be many more dire things happening in the area. We don't want to worry him when we're all safe and unhurt.'

'Quite right, Sister, we'll wait now until

morning,' said Joan.

'There are hot-water bottles in the bottom of the airing cupboard — we haven't had any use for them for ages, but now would seem to be a good time, don't you agree, Mother?' Sister Clare smiled. 'You see, I never throw away anything that might come in handy.'

Joan thought of all the odds and ends in Sister Clare's dresser. 'And how absolutely right you are, my dear,' she said.

'I could wrap up warm and walk up to the farm,' said Sister Emma, her young face bright with excitement, 'and get help!'

'There's no help we really need until morning, Sister,' Joan smiled. 'We'll all manage very well for one night.' She patted Emma's shoulder. 'But thank you, dear, for offering to brave the storm for us. We must pray that the Murrays are all OK.'

'We could have a sing-song,' said Sister Flora, rubbing her hands in the warmth of the fire. 'Like in the wartime.'

'I think,' said Clare, 'some cocoa would be nice and I'm sure I can rustle up some digestive biscuits. Mary, come and give me a hand dear.'

'That would be marvellous, Sister, you'd really lift our spirits if you could do that,' said Joan.

Clare smiled. 'No sooner said than nearly done, Mother. Come child' — she beckoned to Mary — 'I'll teach you how to make real cocoa — none of your instant stuff in my kitchen!'

'You never panic do you?' said Mary.

'My goodness, child — what's to panic about? We've just got tonight to get through and we'll sleep most of that away — and in the morning Bill Murray will arrive on his tractor to check up on us, won't he, Mother?'

'I have no doubt that he will, Sister, no doubt at all,' Joan smiled.

'I wish — I wish that I had friends like that,' Mary said wistfully, 'people I could really trust and rely on.'

'It cuts both ways, child,' said Clare. 'Friends trust and rely on one another. It's not just give and take — it's give and give on all sides. Now then, let's begin with this cocoa to comfort our shivering sisters!' Clare smiled and patted the girl's arm gently. She bustled off in the direction of the kitchen with the torch and a candle, assuring Joan that she had a goodly supply of matches in the dresser drawer. Mary followed close behind her.

Sister Joan went over to the sideboard to replace the notebook neatly beside the now redundant telephone. She thought of the extension in her study, equally useless. Sister Imelda got up from her chair by the fire and came to stand beside her.

'You've found something out, haven't you?' she whispered. 'About the girl? I haven't had a chance to talk to you since we got back from town. I could see you had something on your mind.'

Joan smiled at her. 'How well you know me, Sister.'

'When you went into the *Gazette* office it wasn't to find out about the gardening article that Amy and Louise are going to write, was it?'

'No, Imelda, it wasn't.'

'Then it was about Mary?'

'Yes.'

'She's that missing girl, isn't she! — that singer?'

Joan looked at Imelda gravely. 'We'd make a good pair of sleuths, wouldn't we, Imelda?'

'Well, it all seemed to be making a pattern, Mother — and although it's not my place to interfere without your say-so, I couldn't help my jolly brain piecing it all together, especially after what Len Harvey said to us when we parked on his forecourt this afternoon.'

'I asked the girl in the *Gazette* office to

find the report on Mary's talent show,' Joan admitted. 'I have the print-out, I know exactly who she is — there's even a photo. Oh, Sister, I felt so guilty about doing it; it was so sneaky of me.'

Imelda took her hand. 'With all respect, Mother, rubbish! We can't just bowl along indefinitely with this young lady calling the tune. Now's the time to get some of the mystery sorted. She can't leave — there's a jolly great oak tree blocking the lane. We're all stuck here now until someone comes with a chain saw and cuts it up!'

'You're absolutely right, Imelda,' Joan whispered back. 'Maybe we should pray that Providence doesn't send us someone too soon, so that I can have a good long talk with Mary!'

They both jumped, for at that very moment the doorbell rang.

'Oh dear! Oh lumme!' said Sister Imelda 'We didn't ask Providence quick enough! Who in Heaven's name could that be!'

CHAPTER SEVENTEEN

By the time Joan and Sister Imelda reached the front door, Sister Clare was there already with Mary close beside her.

'It shouldn't be anyone,' Clare whispered. 'The lane is blocked.'

'How did the doorbell ring? There isn't any power — that's spooky!' Mary sounded scared.

'It's got a battery, that's why,' Imelda whispered.

'Why are we all talking like a horror film?' Joan went towards the door. 'There's someone on the outside probably soaking wet and wanting to come in from the cold.'

'Oh, Mother, be careful, it must be someone powerful desperate to come out on a night like this. See if you can see anything through the letterbox.' Sister Clare handed Joan the torch.

Joan opened the flap carefully and shone the torch through. 'There's something black and shiny — that's all I can see. Oh! this is just too silly.' She straightened up and turned the catch on the door opening it to the length of the safety chain. 'Constable Bradley — oh, how glad we are to see you! Come in, you're drenched!' She opened the door wide.

Constable Bradley came into the hall dripping puddles all over the terracotta tiles.

'What a storm!' he said, removing his hat and rain jacket. 'Are you all OK? No one hurt? Mr Murray rang me with his mobile — said all the lines are down. He was checking up on his cows in the shed when the lights went out — took him a while to get the generator going.'

'How did you manage to get here? The lane is blocked — you must have climbed over the fallen tree.' Joan helped him with his wet jacket, draping it over the big carved chair by the door.

'Yes, that's exactly what I did. I had to leave the car on the other side. Don't any of you go near that tree tomorrow. There are wires hanging — very dangerous. I've made contact with the electric people on my mobile they'll be here soon as possible to put things to rights.'

'Oh Constable, that's very kind of you — thank you so much,' said Joan.

'If I could just get hold of a chain saw I could give a hand,' Sister Imelda said eagerly.

'I think, Sister, we'll leave this to the experts. Don't you think that would be wise, Constable?' Joan asked.

'Quite right, Reverend, quite right, but it's brave of you to offer.' He smiled at Imelda who blushed vividly.

'Your roof must have suffered some damage, Reverend. There's a lot of folk in the town with chimneys down and the like.' He removed his wellingtons, leaving them neatly on the doormat.

'I fear so,' said Joan. 'The old bathtub and the buckets in the attic will be full to bursting. That'll be the first job of the morning — emptying it all out.'

'Do you mean you'll have to carry it all the way down the stairs?' asked PC Bradley.

'Oh no,' smiled Sister Imelda. 'We just chuck it out of the attic window!'

'Most enterprising, Sister.' He grinned. 'By the way, Mr Murray thought of your roof — offered a couple of big tarpaulins and a pair of strong lads to fix it up if we get a window in the weather tomorrow. There's probably more storm where this came from — you can't be too careful.'

'That will be a great help and most kind,'

replied Joan. 'Sister Imelda, take PC Bradley along to the living-room and find him a chair by the fire, I'll help with the cocoa.'

'I'm liable to steam a bit,' he said ruefully.

'Not to worry.' Sister Imelda ushered him ahead of her. 'You'll soon dry out.'

The cocoa was hot and welcome. They all sipped quietly by the fire from the big white china mugs.

'My goodness, I've never tasted anything quite so good.' Constable Bradley sat with his hands wrapped around his mug and his feet in thermal socks stretched out to the blaze. 'Except, of course, Sister Clare, your most excellent tea.'

'That's because you needed it badly and it's real cocoa,' Sister Clare nodded wisely.

'I only hope you won't develop rheumatism drying those damp socks like that,' observed Sister Madeline.

Joan noted that he was indeed steaming, quite considerably.

'There's no instant cocoa in Sister Clare's kitchen,' Mary laughed, then paled and seemed to shrink into her chair as the policeman turned to look at her.

'You must be the young visitor with the red Porsche that everyone's talking about. I hear tell that even Sister Imelda has had a drive of it!' he laughed.

Mary sat on the edge of her chair, suddenly on the defensive. 'Yes, it is mine, my Dad gave it to me for my twenty-first birthday. I may look young but I've got a licence and everything and it's OK for Sister to drive it and — and I'm only staying for a little while.' She spoke almost in one breath.

'I'm sure everything is legal, my dear, I wasn't being official,' he said kindly. 'Funny thing, though — a chap came into the police station the other day asking if we'd seen a car of that description. Trouble was, the girl he described as driving it wasn't a bit like you. The girl he was looking for sounded more like a pop star or something — not someone seeking retreat in a convent,' he smiled reasuringly. 'I'm sure she couldn't have helped make cocoa like this.' His eyes twinkled over the edge of his mug as he took another sip.

Constable Bradley was loath to go out into the rain again but, 'Duty calls,' he said, as he put on his hat and jacket and pushed his feet back into his wellies. 'Never fear, Sisters — only one cold night for you we hope, then all will be well.'

They watched from the front door as he got soaked again on his way back to the car on the other side of the fallen oak tree. Joan thought of him backing the vehicle all the way down the lane to the main road, as there was nowhere to turn in the lane. PC Bradley was a good friend. Had he suspected who Mary really was? Her situation was no longer of interest to him officially as she was of age and had made telephone contact with her mother, but he must have had the original message about her disappearance and he was a good policeman. It wouldn't be difficult for him to put two and two together. After all, hadn't she done just that!

Back by the fireside again Sister Clare said, 'More cocoa anyone?' She picked up one of two large white jugs keeping warm on the hearth and offered it. They all took a little more.

It seemed very quiet after PC Bradley had left. Joan looked at them all, sitting at the fireside together. The music was still playing softly on Classic FM, but no one spoke. She felt tired. It had been quite an out-of-the-ordinary day and she felt ready for her bed, cold as her room would be.

'Should we see to the hot water bottles, Sister?' She turned to Clare.

'Yes, Mother, that would be a good idea — there's nothing more we can do now. I'll put aside some kindling and newspaper ready to light the fire in here in the morning.' She began to collect the mugs and jugs together onto a large tray. Mary left her chair and helped her.

Joan felt that suddenly the room was filled with warmth and love. Now would be the time, she thought, now is the moment, I musn't lose it, or let it pass. Tomorrow will be hectic with a dozen and more things to do — there will be no moment like this.

'I have something important to say to all of you and I think it should be now while we're here together.' Joan could see that Mary had paled. She had moved to the door carrying the tray. 'No, Mary, leave that on the table and come back here to the fire.' The girl did as she was told, hesitatingly. Joan knew instinctively that Mary was aware of what was to be said.

'You're going to tell them, aren't you?' Sister Imelda, standing beside Joan, whispered softly.

Joan nodded. 'Sisters, I have to tell you that the child here with us, who came to us out of just such a storm as tonight and who we know as Mary Winter, is, in fact, not Mary Winter at all.' She turned to Mary. 'I think, my dear, you owe it to us all to admit who you really are.' She reached out and took the girl's hand in hers.

Mary looked at her with resignation in her

eyes. Then, facing the sisters, she sighed and said, 'First of all, I know you're my friends and I need friends very much.' She took a deep breath. 'I'm Rebecca Marie Thornton.'

The nuns remained silent glancing at one another in puzzled silence. Mary's brave statement seemed to mean nothing at all to them.

Mary smiled. 'I mean, I'm Beccy-Marie, Gucci Foot — you know, the girl who was reported missing on the radio that I-I smashed.'

Sister Emma took a step forward. 'You-you mean, you're the pop star whose picture's on the keyring?'

'Yes.'

'Oh golly!' She turned to Joan. 'Oh, Mother, we've got a celebrity!' Then, gazing again at Mary, 'So, that's why you cut all your hair off and your sparkly nails too. So that you could hide! Oh my, this is all so exciting!'

'You're a naughty girl.' Sister Clare wagged a finger at Mary. 'How did you suppose we could do anything for you if we didn't know your troubles? Sure you can't stay here without becoming almost one of the family. We were bound to be curious about you. The good Lord love us, we've been falling over ourselves to help you, after all — that's what we're here for!'

Joan smiled to herself. Dear Sister Clare, she thought, I couldn't have put it better myself.

Suddenly the room was filled with chatter, questions flowing so fast that Joan realized Mary was becoming quite confused. She held up her hands.

'Sisters, Sisters, please! There's another day tomorrow. Give Mary — or should I say Rebecca — some peace, for that is what she's seeking, I believe. I'm sure that now the ice is broken and her secret is out we can give her all the support she needs whatever her story is. Now, it's time for prayers and bed. The morning will come with a new day for all of us.'

'I-I just want to say thank you to everyone. I've been such a pain, I know. And — please don't stop calling me Mary. It sort of makes me feel that I fit in somehow.'

'Well,' said Sister Clare, 'that's a lot more acceptable than Gucci Foot. How did you come by such a funny name anyway?'

'Oh, it's my sandals! You know, the high-heeled pink ones with all the glitter on. They're made specially for me by Gucci. Mum orders them for me from Italy.'

'Hrrrumph!' snorted Sister Clare. 'That's an awful long way to go for such discomfort!

Sure, mine are plain, comfortably flat and local. Come along child and help me with this washing-up for I can't abide it to be there facing me in the morning. We can sort out those hot water bottles, too — I think there's enough to go around.'

Mary carried the tray and followed Clare, who preceded her with the torch, in the direction of the kitchen.

'Well,' said Madeline quietly, 'that was a revelation! How long have you known, Mother?'

Joan proceeded to tell the whole story, eventually saying, 'If she's just a pop star feeling a bit jaded with the whole rat race of the entertainment world, then it's not such an earth-shattering thing after all. We should be able to cope with that when things have been explained to the parents. The whole episode must be creating havoc with their engagement timetable as well as worrying them half to death.'

Sister Madeline sighed. 'I still have a feeling that all is not well with the child's health. Maybe now she'll feel free to tell us eveything. She's ailing in some way. I have a feeling about it. She loses colour so quickly. Probably the dieting, stage appearances, travelling here, there and all over the place — it seems to tie in with her delicate condition. Time will tell, I suppose, although I'd dearly like Doctor Stewart to have a look at her. However, Sister Clare will find a way of nourishing her whether she wants it or not.'

'Until the oak tree is cleared away Doctor Stewart is out of the question and I think Mary would have something quite vehement to say about that anyway. She's a very independent little soul,' Joan said.

'I'd have thought she'd have to be quite a toughie to do a job like that! But it explains the posh car and the money, doesn't it?' said Imelda, making a face. 'I wouldn't last a week at the job!' She laughed. 'Can you imagine me, being a pop star?'

'We wouldn't want to part with you, Imelda, even if the greatest impresario in the world discovered your talents. We need you here to keep our spirits up.' Joan smiled as they all agreed.

'And — who else but you could keep the "jolly" boiler going?' added Madeline.

'So, Mary's got nothing to do with the Mafia after all.' Sister Emma sounded almost disappointed.

A feeling of relief came over Joan which almost outweighed her weariness. Her Sisters' cheeks were rosy with laughter despite the wind and the rain lashing against the windows, the expected cold of the night and the reality of a heavy day on the morrow. She thought of Mary in the kitchen with Sister Clare, helping with the washing-up and the hot-water bottles. So, after all, her name was Rebecca Marie Thornton, famous pop star — but if it really were Mary Winter, would she not be the same girl, sent to them in a storm for protection and care?

CHAPTER EIGHTEEN

Although she was very weary, it wasn't easy to get to sleep. Curled up in her woollen dressing gown and cuddling her hot water bottle, Sister Joan's mind raced with the excitement of the day. The room was cold and condensation began to gather on the inside of the window which faced the back garden and the sea. Soon drowsiness overcame her whirling brain and she began to slip into the first delight of unconsiousness, that limbo between sleeping and waking when the body is relaxed and warm and ready to give up the cares of the day.

'Sister!'

The voice had a far-away, dream-like quality — how nice, I'm begining to dream, Joan thought.

'Sister!'

The voice came again, clearer and accompanied by a tapping at her door. She opened her eyes. 'Who is it? What's wrong?'

'It's me, Sister — it's Mary. Can I come in? Please, it's ever so urgent!'

Joan sat up in bed still clutching the hot-water bottle. 'Of course, dear — come in.'

The door opened and the girl entered, muffled up in a large aging dressing gown that could only have belonged to Sister Imelda, and wearing the woolly hat with 'I Hate Cold Weather' embroidered on it. 'I looked out of my window,' she said, 'it's not raining and the wind has stopped.' Her eyes were wide as with one hand she clutched the dressing gown closer around her body. In the other she carried a candle in a white enamel holder.

'Mary, you should be in bed. You'd be nice and warm by now if you'd stayed there. Now it's going to take you an age to get cosy again.'

'I looked out of my window.'

'Mary!'

'Please listen to me, Sister. I could see the old apple tree in the garden.'

'Mary, you're over excited — go back to your bed at once you silly girl. It's not the time for admiring the winter garden — unless that tree has blown down too.'

'Sister Joan, there's a man standing underneath it!'

Suddenly Joan was wide awake. She sat

bolt upright in her bed. 'Mary — you must have been half asleep, dear girl. How could there possibly be a man under the apple tree?'

'I haven't been asleep yet. I just couldn't close my eyes for thinking about what that policeman said about me and the car. So I opened the window a little bit to see if I could hear the sea. It was just something to do and I couldn't be any colder. These bedrooms are a bit high up but I could see a man underneath the tree.' She held out a hand to Joan. 'Sister, you can see the garden from here — you're just next door to me. Come and look.'

Joan got out of bed and went to the window. Mary came and stood beside her. 'There's no one there, Mary, nobody at all. You're imagining things — it's been a hard day.'

'No, I'm not — look there — look now!' she pointed. 'See!' Mary rubbed a circle of condensation off the window.

As Joan looked through, she saw a flare of light and the soft glow of a cigarette. Illuminated in the glare of the match was the face of a man. She drew the curtains together quickly, her heart beating rapidly, and she pulled Mary away from the window. 'Don't look again — we may be seen.'

'Is it PC Bradley? Do you think he's come back to see if we're OK?' Mary's voice was shaking.

Sister Joan took hold of the girl's shoulders gently. 'Now, Mary, all the doors are locked. We're quite safe if we stay where we are. Go quietly and get your mobile and we'll phone the police. PC Bradley gave up smoking two years ago — it isn't possible that it could be him out there.' Her hands shook as she lit the candle beside her bed.

When Mary hurried off to get the phone Joan peeped through the curtains again. Although she couldn't see the outline of the man against the dark of the tree she could still see the occasional glow of his cigarette. Just before Mary returned even that had disappeared.

'Is he still there — have you looked?' Mary put down her candle, operated the phone and held it to her ear.

'I-I think he's still there,' said Joan. 'But I can't see the light from his cigarette any more.'

Mary spoke into the phone. 'Police, please, quickly! Oh! quickly, please. . . . Police? Yes, there's a man prowling around outside . . . the convent — yes, the Stella Maris Convent . . . please come quickly — we don't know what to do . . . yes, we're all locked, but the power's off and we've got no lights . . . oh hurry . . . thank you . . . oh thank you!' She switched off the phone. 'They're coming right away.'

'Thank God.' Joan began to feel cold. 'I don't think we should waken the other sisters, they'd be frightened. Maybe he won't try to break in. It's all very quiet. We'll just wait. It's all we can do.' She sat on the bed and Mary came and sat close beside her, both of them clutching their hot-water bottles and waiting for any sound.

The night was quiet now, the storm had passed and Joan felt that she could almost touch the silence it was so profound.

'What's going on — someone sick?' Sister Imelda put her head around the door. She had on her purple anorak and the hood was pulled close around her face. 'Mary not well?' she asked, as she came into the room.

'We've got a prowler — in the garden under the apple tree! I've just phoned the police. They'll be here soon.' Mary moved up to make a space for Imelda to sit on the bed.

'A what?'

Together they told her what they'd seen through the window.

'Well! That's all we need. I'll go up to the attic and fetch that old hockey stick. If he decides to break in he'll have to get past me first! Fancy, a burglar on a night like this! They never miss an opportunity do they? I'll jolly stop him, see if I don't!'

'No, Sister, just stay here with us. We don't want to disturb the others if we can help it. We must leave it all to the police.' Joan reached over Mary to put a restraining hand on Imelda's arm. 'Remember, you're a nun.'

'Yes, Mother, of course, but I don't like feeling so helpless.'

'Well, he hasn't done anything yet except stand under the tree smoking a cigarette and if the worst comes to the worst there's only one of him and eight of us!'

'Nine!' said Mary.

'We won't hear them come — the police,' said Imelda. 'They're going to have to climb over the oak tree to get to us.'

They sat together on Sister Joan's bed and waited in the silence. It seemed like an eternity.

'I don't think they're coming,' Mary began to sob. 'They think it's all a hoax.'

Joan put her arm around the girl. 'They'll come — just you wait and see, they'll not let us down.'

'But it's taking so long. . . .'

The doorbell rang.

'They're here.' Sister Imelda got up and

made for the door. 'I'll let them in.'

'Oh, don't, Sister — it might be the prowler.' Mary made to stop her.

'Prowlers don't ring doorbells.' Imelda went out onto the landing and made her way down the stairs followed closely by Sister Joan and Mary.

Imelda stooped and opened the letterbox. 'Who is it?' she shouted through it.

'Police — it's Constable Bradley — all's well, Sisters — we've caught him, you can open the door.'

Imelda did so immediately. Four policemen, including PC Bradley, stood on the doorstep. A man was there with them, with his hands secured behind his back.

'We'll come in if we may,' said PC Bradley.

Imelda opened the door wider and they came in. Joan, hearing a sound behind her, glanced up the stairs to see the other nuns leaning over the landing rail, dressed in an assortment of warm clothing and looking very puzzled. So much for not disturbing the others, she thought.

'We found him just outside in the drive, Reverend Mother. His car was in the lane — he must have climbed over the tree like we had to,' PC Bradley said. 'He said he weren't doing anything.'

The young man who was hanging his head looked up pleadingly. 'I wasn't — I really wasn't doing any harm. You don't have to put handcuffs on me. I-I was looking for someone. I've been looking for days and days. . . .'

Joan suddenly felt Mary's hand grip her arm until it hurt. She saw the girl's ashen face as she recognized the young man.

'Allan!' Mary shouted.

Sister Imelda caught her as she fainted. Lowering her gently to the floor she looked up at Sister Joan. 'Good grief!' she exclaimed, 'it must be the jolly boyfriend!'

CHAPTER NINETEEN

Sister Joan knelt beside Mary and patted her hand. She was relieved to see Sister Madeline hurrying down the stairs to join them.

'Bring her upstairs to her bed, right away!' Madeline's voice had an authority that she had never used in the presence of her Superior on any other occasion.

Sister Imelda lifted the girl as if she were a child and carried her towards the stairs followed closely by Madeline.

Suddenly Joan felt quite helpless but became aware that although she was Reverend Mother she had with her the strength of all her Sisters. She stood up and faced the young man who looked at her with anxiety in his eyes.

'So,' she asked softly, 'you are Allan?'

'Yes, madam,' he replied politely. 'Beccy just fainted, didn't she? She will be OK won't she?'

'Yes, it was just a shock, seeing you suddenly like that. Sister Madeline will take care of her.' Dear God, she thought, please let it be only that.

'Well!' PC Bradley stepped forward. 'We'll see about getting that tree cleared — or at least enough of it to get the doctor through tonight. I gather you'll be needing him?'

'Oh yes, Constable, thank you — we certainly will. Mary has no say in the matter now.'

PC Bradley released Allan from the handcuffs. 'I certainly realize who you are, sir, and I don't believe you're of any danger to these good ladies.'

Joan was surprised. 'But how . . . ?'

'We've known all along about your visitor. All police stations were notified countrywide,' he said. 'Fact is, the search was called off as soon as we were informed that the girl was safe and had phoned home. As the boyfriend here had been found and she is of age, we had no right to interfere. The jazzy sandal was a dead giveaway and cutting all that lovely hair off — what a waste. Poor lass, she must be properly scared half out of her wits about something or other. I hope things can be sorted out now. We can help, too, you know — if you need us. It's not all cops and robbers in this job.' He grinned and leaned towards Joan. 'You didn't think that a nun driving a bright red Porsche would go quite unnoticed, did you? Half the town are talking about it. I hope now that you'll contact the parents, Reverend Mother, and put their minds at rest. We've been keeping a friendly eye on you, you know.' He winked.

'Oh, Constable Bradley, we should have guessed.' Joan put her hand on his arm. 'It's just all been so unusual for us — it was difficult to know what to do. Mary was so determined to hide. Why, we even hid the Porsche in the barn under a tarpaulin, in case, well, in case she was being threatened by gangsters — or someone,' she ended lamely.

PC Bradley smiled. 'We know you did. You've been safer than you realized you know.' He turned to Allan, 'Now, young man — there's nothing more you can do tonight. We'll leave your car here and you can come home with me. We've got a spare room, the missus and me, and I'll bring you back in the morning in the proper manner.'

'But I want to see Beccy now!' the young man pleaded.

'I have no doubt that you have a lot to say to her — but now is not the time. Come on, sir, I don't want to have to feel your collar again tonight!'

Allan persisted, 'But, I'm booked into a bed and breakfast. . . .'

'I'd be glad if you'd come with me, sir. I'll rest easy if I know where you are. Be assured that it's not custody that I'm taking you into, for I'm sure that Reverend Mother doesn't want to press charges under the circumstances?' He looked at Joan for approval.

'Oh! Of course not. Please take him home, Constable, then we can all get a good night's sleep — and thank you so much for being so understanding.'

'Not at all, Sister.' PC Bradley took Allan by the arm and led him to the front door. Allan turned and faced Joan before he went through.

'I-I'm sorry,' he said, 'to have frightened you like that. But — I had to see Beccy — I just had to. I love her so much . . . something happened . . . she didn't understand . . . why do you call her Mary?'

'Come along now, sir, there'll be plenty of time for all that tomorrow. The Reverend has a lot to do and much to think about. The other officers will arrange to have the tree cleared and I shall phone the doctor myself, don't you worry about a thing.'

'Thank you so much, Constable.' Joan felt

relief to know that Doctor Stewart would be with them in a short while. She could hardly wait to get upstairs to see Mary.

Joan bade them goodnight and closed the big front door softly behind them. She had no need to be quiet because all the sisters began to chatter as she made her way up the stairs.

'Hush!' she held up her hand. 'Go back to your beds before they're quite cold. There's another day tomorrow and plenty of time for questions then.'

Joan felt very weary as she sat in Mary's room with Sister Madeline and Imelda while they waited for Doctor Stewart. Although she opened her eyes after a while the girl's face was very pale. They heard the arrival of the team sent to clear the tree and the sound of chainsaws cutting through the darkness as well as the tree.

'There's the doorbell,' Imelda said. 'That'll be the doctor, I'll go and let him in.'

Joan was relieved to hear Doctor Stewart's heavy footsteps coming up the stairs and the sound of his voice as he spoke to Imelda.

'Well now, what have we here?' Doctor Stewart's soft Scottish accent warmed Joan's heart and brought a sense of security back to her world. Sitting on the edge of Mary's bed, he put his bag down on the floor beside it.

Mary had woken but was looking quite confused. 'I — think I passed out. . . .'

Doctor Stewart put his hand on her forehead. 'Hush now — we've plenty of time to find out what the trouble is. Sister Madeline, will you stay here, please? Sisters Joan and Imelda — it would be a good idea for you to go downstairs, find the warmest spot, and wait for me there. I'll be down as soon as I've had a word with this young lady. Then — a cup of tea would be most welcome.'

Joan and Imelda, after going to the kitchen to put the big kettle on the Rayburn, returned to the living-room and sat by the fire. Imelda put a couple of logs on the dying embers and soon a warm blaze illuminated the room. The flames cast shadows over the ceiling.

'She's very ill, isn't she?' Imelda said softly. 'A girl these days doesn't just faint away like that for nothing — not even seeing the missing boyfriend all of a sudden. Going by what she's said about him already, like never wanting to see him again — why, she should have been more angry than anything.'

'I've been worried for quite some time, Imelda,' Joan sighed. 'So has Madeline — and she's the one with all the experience. Doctor Stewart will soon discover what's wrong with Mary. But, oh my! What a busy day it will be for us all tomorrow.'

'May I come in, Sisters?' Doctor Stewart tapped on the door and entered. 'Nice blaze you have in here; it's a mite chilly upstairs.'

'Oh Doctor, how is Mary? Is she very ill?' Joan clasped her hands together nervously.

'Well' — Doctor Stewart held his hands out to the fire — 'she's awful skinny and dieted to a shred, but she's a tough little thing considering the life she leads. Oh yes, she's told me all. My own children are great fans and I approve — she's a good role model, no drink or drugs — a good girl for all her noisy music. What she needs is nourishment and rest. I've given her a good examination and as far as I can tell she's quite OK — just very overwrought.' He rubbed his warmed hands together. 'And — I'm sure you'll be glad to know — although I'd like her to come to the hospital as soon as possible for a scan — her baby will be fine, too.'

Nothing was said — not even, 'Oh dear. Oh lumme!'

Joan was so glad that she was still sitting down.

CHAPTER TWENTY

The only sound that broke the silence in the room was the crackling of the logs in the fireplace. Doctor Stewart continued to warm his hands, seemingly unaware of the shock he had caused the two sisters. Joan realized that her mouth was still hanging open with surprise and — glancing at Sister Imelda — noticed that she was very pale.

Madeline stepped forward and took Joan's hand. 'Mother?' she said anxiously. 'Oh Mother, I know how you feel. It wasn't such a shock to me. You see, I suspected but, I-I didn't want to say anything before Mary bucked up enough courage to tell you. I could have been quite wrong, of course.'

Doctor Stewart turned away from the fire. 'Do you mean you didn't know about the girl's condition?' He looked at Madeline. 'You didn't turn a hair when I made my diagnosis upstairs. The lass has known all along, of course. But I had no idea she'd not told you.'

'She's admitted to a lot of things,' said Joan, 'and she's been pale and listless, her appetite has been erratic but she's never mentioned a-a —'

'A jolly baby!' gasped Sister Imelda.

Joan's mouth had become very dry. 'My legs feel wobbly,' she whispered to Sister Madeline.

'Nice cup of tea — that's what we all need.' Doctor Stewart rubbed his hands together. 'Perfectly natural thing you know, dear lady.' He addressed Joan. 'The lass is not ill and she'll only be queasy for a little while longer.' He frowned. 'There'll be a man in the picture somewhere, of course. It would be well if he was involved as soon as possible. Knowing who the lass is, I can see that this state of affairs will make great changes to her life. Now, where's my favourite tea-maker?'

'I'm here.' Sister Clare's head and one shoulder appeared around the door.

'I'm sorry I didn't stay in my bed, Mother — I couldn't settle. I had to come down to see if all was well.'

'Did you hear?' Joan asked.

'Yes, Mother. I wasn't being nosy. I was going to suggest some tea.' Her usual rosy cheeks were ashen.

'Oh please, Clare — it couldn't be more welcome.' This new challenge was beginning to feel like a heavy weight in Joan's heart.

Sister Joan climbed the stairs and went into the girl's room. Putting a mug of tea on the side table she sat down wearily on the bed.

'Mary? Oh Mary,' she sighed.

The girl, her cropped fair hair sticking up all over her head like down on a summer dandelion, turned her head on the pillow and faced the wall. 'That's it, isn't it?' she said softly. 'I told you there'd be something you'd throw me out for. This is it. You've got no choice now, have you? You nuns can't be lumbered with a problem like this.'

'You believe it to be a problem, do you?'

'Yes.'

'Mary, bringing a child into the world is one of the most wonderful things a woman can do. Your condition is the most important thing in the world to us and certainly no reason to deny you both shelter and understanding, if that's what you need. Your child is no problem. Don't worry, we'll sort something out between us.'

Mary turned her head and looked at Joan. Tears streamed down her small face and dampened the pillow. She reached out her hand and Joan clasped it in both of hers.

'Thank you, Sister,' Mary whispered. 'I made the mistake of thinking that if I tried to ignore the baby, it would go away. But, it won't, will it? It's — it's really going to happen, isn't it?'

'Yes, Mary, there are not many things in life that are more real than this. It will be a big responsibility for you, but you must never forget that a baby is a gift. Your boyfriend, Allan, does he know?'

'Yes.' Mary released Joan's hand.

'Had he nothing to say when you told him about it?'

'I phoned him when I found out — about the baby. He sounded so excited and happy. That's why I didn't understand when. . . .' She paused. 'He said he'd come over directly — Mum and Dad were away. I was on my own. I waited and waited — he didn't turn up. I got in the car and went over to his flat. He wasn't there. I went back home. He still didn't come, so I got in a panic, packed a bag with my phone and stuff, got a lot of money out of the cash machine, filled the car with petrol and just took off! I must have been crazy!' she sighed. 'You know the rest.'

'What did you think you could achieve by doing all that?' Joan asked quietly. 'This is a situation, Mary, from which you cannot run.'

'I know — I just didn't know what to do, or how to tell Mum and Dad — well, everything. It was true when I told you I needed some space to think what to do next. You must have wondered what on earth was the matter with me.'

'Sister Madeline suspected.'

'She would!' Mary said quietly.

'She didn't say a word at the time. She hoped that if she was right you'd tell us yourself. Anyway, Allan is coming here in the morning, we'll talk then. Things must be sorted out — this is all very serious, my dear.'

'I won't talk to him!' Mary said angrily. 'He promised to love me for ever — now he doesn't want me, he ran out on me. I needed him so much and he didn't turn up.'

'There could have been many reasons for his not doing so, Mary. You must hear him out.'

'It was only a ten-minute drive from his flat to our house. He just chickened out, that's what!' She turned her face to the wall again.

Joan sighed. 'He says he loves you. After all, he did come searching for you.' She smiled. 'He even got himself handcuffed in the effort.'

'I don't care — I won't see him!' Mary was adamant.

'Oh yes you jolly will!' My goodness, thought Joan, I'm begining to sound like Sister Imelda. 'Now, drink that tea then settle down to sleep. There's not much left of the night so we'd better make the most of it — there's another day tomorrow.' She stood up and began to tuck Mary in.

The girl suddenly sat up, flung both arms around Joan's neck and pressed her face against her cheek. 'Oh Sister Joan!'

'What is it, dear?'

'I want my Mum!'

CHAPTER
TWENTY-ONE

The lane that led from the convent to the main road was filled with the noise of men clearing what remained of the old tree and putting the fallen wires to rights. Bill Murray and two hefty lads arrived from the farm on a tractor pulling a trailer containing ladders, tarpaulins and tools to see to the roof as promised. He also supplied Sister Clare with a small churn of milk and two oven-ready chickens that he declared were surplus to his requirements. 'You'll be doing me a good turn if you'd dispose of 'em for me,' he had said.

Mary sat on the edge of her chair in Sister Joan's study, clutching her mobile phone almost as if it gave her some sort of comfort.

'We shall now phone your parents and tell them exactly where you are,' said Joan.

'Oh Sister — I-I can't. . . .'

'As our telephone is not yet connected, you can press the buttons on your mobile and I'll do the talking.' Joan felt strangely relieved to have something positive to do after all the cloak and dagger nightmares with Mary. 'I shall talk to them and arrange for them to come here.' A look of sheer panic crossed the girl's face. 'I shall be with you all the time, Mary — you've nothing to fear,' she said gently.

'They're going to be spitting mad!' said Mary. ' 'Specially Mum!'

'No they're not, dear — they're going to be very relieved.'

Joan was perfectly right. It took only a few minutes to explain where Mary was.

Mrs Thornton knew exactly where to find them. 'Why didn't I realize?' she said. 'We had such happy times at Compton Bay in the old days. I should have known where to look. Is my Beccy OK? She's not hurt is she?' Mary's mother was tearful as she said goodbye and rang off. Joan hadn't told her about the baby. That was for Mary to do and anyway, the telephone just didn't seem to be the proper way to deliver such news.

'They'll be here as soon as they can,' she said handing the mobile back to Mary. 'The lane's nearly cleared, PC Bradley will be here soon with Allan. We'll have plenty of time to have a talk with him before your parents get here — it will be a long drive

244

for them. Your mother said they'll spend the night at a hotel in town.'

Mary stood up. 'I'm going to my room — there's no way I'm going to talk to Allan!'

'I think, Mary, it's time for you to behave like a grownup and not like a spoilt child,' Joan said angrily. 'I believe that you're mature enough to speak sensibly to your baby's father. You must realize that the little one's future is at stake and he or she must have your total consideration. The baby is the important one in all this!'

Mary sat down again. She looked so young, so vulnerable — so thin. She needed love, security and nourishment now, more than money and fame, thought Joan. A baby? Why! she was not much more than a baby herself. Even though she'd been given a Porsche for her twenty-first birthday.

Mary looked at Joan, her large blue eyes dominating her small face. 'You're absolutely right, Sister,' she said quietly. 'I've been selfish — but I still don't want to talk to him!'

Joan heard the familiar sound of sister Clare's knuckles tapping on the study door. 'Come in, Sister.'

Clare opened the door. 'It's PC Bradley, Mother and — and — the other gentleman.' She ushered them in and left, closing the door quietly behind her.

'Good morning, Reverend. I've brought the young man as promised.'

'Thank you, Constable,' Joan smiled.

The policeman moved awkwardly from one foot to the other. 'Well then, I'll be leaving you to it,' he said. 'I shall be in the kitchen for a while if needed, then I have to be going — on duty, you understand.' He left the room quietly, his official hat tucked neatly under his arm.

'Oh Beccy! Are you OK?' Allan moved towards the girl.

'Fat lot you care!' She turned away from him.

'I do care — I've been worried half to death about you!'

'You didn't turn up — after I phoned — you didn't come!' She fiddled with a pen on the desk.

Joan supressed a look of surprise — this was the girl who didn't want to talk.

'Mary, please let me explain —'

She spun around to face him. 'No! There isn't an excuse in the world that'll get me to forgive you!'

'Mary! Don't shout. Remember where you are,' said Joan softly. 'We must give Allan a chance — hear what he has to say.'

'Sorry, Sister.' Mary lowered her eyes. 'Go

on, then — I'm listening,' she said grudgingly.

'Please sit down, Allan.' Joan indicated the other chair in front of her desk. 'Just relax and tell Mary — er, Rebecca, exactly why you appeared to have deserted her.'

Allan sat down. 'I would never desert her, madam — I love her. Beccy, you know that!' He leaned across and put out his hand to Mary. She made no attempt to proffer hers. He sat back in the chair again and sighed. 'When you phoned me on that Friday morning I was so happy. I knew we'd have to tell your folks — well, everything and that things would be difficult, but I love you so much and I wanted to be with you forever and this — well, this seemed to bring things to a head and out into the open.'

'Then why didn't you turn up?' Mary's voice was more calm and Joan noticed that she was prepared to listen.

'Beccy, my car was in the garage for a service. I just grabbed some notes and loose change, stuffed them in my pocket and ran outside to get a taxi. The next thing I remember was waking up in hospital. I'd been right out of it for a couple of days. No one knew who I was because I had no identity on me — even I didn't know who I was for a few hours. Beccy — I'm so sorry, I didn't see the car coming — just the taxi on the other side of the road. I just wanted to get to you so fast.' He put out his hand again and this time Mary took it and squeezed it hard.

'You're right silly, you.' Her eyes filled with tears. 'You could have been killed, you big dafty! Then I'd have lost you forever. You sure you're OK now?'

'All the better for seeing you again, Beccy.'

They looked into each other's eyes. Sister Joan suddenly got the feeling that she really shouldn't be there at all. She coughed politely. 'So — I gather all is forgiven and you're glad you gave Allan the chance to explain?'

'Oh, yes.' Mary was smiling. 'I wish I hadn't done a runner now!'

Joan sighed. Oh, Mary, she thought, there will be so many people who will wish that. She watched the young couple holding hands as if they never wanted to let go. However, Mary, she thought, if I hadn't found you on that stormy night and brought you home, our lives would just have drifted on and we would only have been immersed in our own troubles. Since you arrived we've all discovered more about ourselves than we had ever realized. I've found strength by

248

trying to help you find yours. She opened the top drawer of her desk to get a tissue — there were the think tank papers. Their own worries were still with them. She hoped that Mary would go away and be happy but she and the sisters would be left to tackle the problems that the modern world had thrust upon them. She blinked hard and blew her nose.

'Now,' she said, 'your parents will be here sometime this evening, Mary. We shall have lunch together and Allan can meet the Sisters.' She smiled. 'I'm sure their curiosity can't be contained for much longer. Then maybe you would both like to take a walk down on the beach. The weather has cleared and there's no cold wind now — it would do you both a lot of good — give you time to talk. I'm sure you have a lot to discuss.'

'Is it lunchtime already?' Mary was still gazing into Allan's eyes. 'Are you hungry?' she asked.

'Ravenous,' he replied, 'despite Mrs Bradley's hearty breakfast.'

Mary got up from her chair and, bending over him, she took his face in her hands and kissed him. 'Allan — oh Allan, I nearly lost you,' she said softly.

'Why do they call you Mary?' Allan whispered.

'It's a long story — but I've got plenty of time to tell you now,' Mary replied.

Joan felt tears pricking her eyelids. That baby's going to have lovely parents, she thought, then — oh my goodness, if Sister Imelda were here she'd say, 'But what about the jolly wedding!'

Allan was still at the convent when Mary's parents arrived. They were nervous and greeted Joan with unecessary reverence when she went to the door with Sister Clare to let them in.

'Oh, you poor souls,' Sister Clare fussed. 'You'll be dying for a hot drink. Shall they come into the kitchen, Mother — it's more cosy in there?'

Of course, Clare was right — they shouldn't stand on ceremony at a time like this. Clare's kitchen was the warmest place to be at ease and talk. 'Lead the way, Sister,' she said.

Sister Clare laughed as she preceded them. 'The kitchen is the heart of the home is it not? Your daughter's there already with her young man. I know she'll be delighted to see you.' Clare was happy and excited.

As they reached the door, Mrs Thornton drew back and put her hand on Joan's arm. 'I-I won't know what to say,' she whispered nervously. 'How on earth did Allan manage to find Beccy?'

'Don't worry,' Joan smiled. 'You'll know just what to say when you see her and they'll both tell you the whole story.' I must make quite sure that the Thorntons are sitting down before they do, she thought.

Clare opened the door and the warmth of the kitchen billowed out into the hall, accompanied by the smell of fresh baked scones and the fragrant promise of a hearty evening meal.

'Mum — oh, Mum.' Mary rushed across the room into her mother's arms nearly bowling her over. 'And Dad — you're here too. Oh, I'm so glad to see you both!'

'Beccy are you all right? Whatever happened? We didn't know where to look. We were so very worried.' The words just spilled over and everyone began talking at once.

So much for not knowing what to say, thought Joan.

Mary's adventure was told around the kitchen table while Allan explained how he'd guessed that she would go back to Compton Bay. 'She never stopped talking about those family holidays!' he laughed. 'Once I got here, well, it isn't every day that nuns are reported to be driving around in a red Porsche!'

Mary's parents filled in the details of their side of the story.

'I didn't hire a private detective after all,' said Mrs Thornton. 'Dad didn't approve. He said to wait till you'd sorted out whatever was troubling you. It was wonderful when you phoned that first time and we knew that wherever you were, you were OK. But just the same a lot of shows have had to be cancelled — I don't think we've slept much and the whole thing has caused a lot of gossip in the press.'

Everything came out into the open except the news of the baby. Suddenly, Joan thought, it was the only information left to tell. There was an awkward pause in the conversation that needed to be filled.

Then Mary's mother said, 'But why was Allan rushing around to our house in the first place, Beccy? It must have been urgent — to get himself knocked over in the attempt! We've heard the story since the Sisters found you, but why were you running away? Was it the pressure of work? There are a lot of things I don't understand, dear.'

Mary's face that had been so bright with excitement, paled a little. She glanced at Allan. 'We have to tell them,' she said quietly.

The kitchen door opened and Imelda

came in, saw the visitors, obviously guessed who they were and before Joan could hold up her hand to stop her she said, 'Oh, how wonderful — the parents, you're here at last. They must have told you the news — jolly exciting, isn't it!'

'Tell us what?' Mary's mother looked puzzled.

'Oh lumme — I've put my foot in it, haven't I?' Imelda looked in desperation at Joan.

'Yes, dear, I do believe you have,' said Joan.

'What's all this about?' Mr Thornton asked.

'Well. . . .' Mary's voice was almost inaudible. 'You see . . . the reason why I ran when I thought Allan had left me was . . . I didn't know what to do because —'

Allan took her hand. 'We're going to have a baby,' he said quietly.

There was a stunned silence.

'More tea — I'll make more tea.' Sister Clare picked up the kettle and hurried to the sink to fill it.

'Not now, Clare dear — not now,' said Joan softly.

The three nuns became as silent as if they were not in the room at all.

Joan could see the tears start in Mrs

Thornton's eyes. 'Beccy — oh, Beccy!'

'I knew you'd be cross!' Mary got up from her chair. 'It's the publicity, isn't it? Pop star expecting baby — shows cancelled — lets down fans — career over — parents angry — you're spitting mad, aren't you!'

'Rebecca Marie — sit down at once and don't talk to your mother like that!' Mr Thornton's strong but firm voice quietened Mary for a while and she sat down again.

'I'm sorry, but it'll stir things up a bit, won't it? A lot of things will have to be put on hold until — until our baby's here. A lot of money will be lost — gigs cancelled, theatre managers angry. How — how will we even begin to sort it all out?' She reached out to clasp Allan's hand.

'It'll be a bit of a nightmare, no doubt.' Her father smiled a little. 'You must realize what a shock this is to us, Beccy. It's going to take a lot of getting used to. However, you hit the nail on the head when you said "our baby", for that's just what he or she will be. A person who belongs to us all. Rebecca, my love, you're entitled to a life.' He turned to his wife. 'Don't you agree, my dear?'

'Of course — Rebecca, it'll be OK, really it will.' There was a sob in Mrs Thornton's voice. 'Sometimes these things happen to

254

change our lives for the best. It's obvious that you love one another dearly, but you should have confided in us, dear — really you should!' Mrs Thornton dabbed at her eyes with a tissue, thoughtfully provided by Sister Clare. 'Oh golly! I'm far too young to be a grandma!'

'But you were never there, Mum,' said Mary softly. 'You were always in some sort of conference with financial advisers, or away arranging new concerts in different countries. When I found out about the baby and phoned Allan, you were both in Japan! I didn't know how to tell you.'

'Oh, Beccy — do you feel that you can't talk to us any more? We love you so dearly — just as much as always.'

'Things changed a lot after I won the talent contest all those years ago. I seemed to become — just a business. I felt I was drifting further and further away from you both. It got harder to tell you how I really felt about things.'

'Beccy, we're so sorry, we didn't mean for things to turn out like this. It's just that the whole thing accelerated into a mad whirl. We thought you were happy — we thought you wanted to go along with it, dear.'

'I do, Mum — it's just the pace. I wanted to slow down a bit, sing things with a bit more meaning. Those awful sandals, I know you had the buckles decorated with diamonds and they're worth a fortune but — they're crippling you know! I'm not sixteen any more. But the money and everything — I felt I couldn't stop. Then' — she looked at the young man holding her hand — 'I met Allan.'

'Well, we knew you were seeing Allan — that was nice. Your father and I liked him very much and you seemed to be happy. Everything seemed — fine. We just didn't realize it had all gone as far as — this!' Mary's mother took a sip of tea.

Joan did the same — her mouth was feeling rather dry too. Diamond buckles on the sandals — and Sister Clare had nearly thrown them away! So — that's why Mary had been almost fanatical about them. There was a long silence.

'Well, it has gone that far, Mum, and there's no running away from it any more,' Mary said quietly, glancing at Joan.

'My dear.' Mrs Thornton leaned towards Mary. 'We love you — you didn't have to run at all you know, but — but —'

'Yes, Mum?'

'There's something very, very important that we must talk about immediately! I know that nowadays a lot of the old values are ignored, but I feel I have to say — to ask you —' She faltered.

'So — when's the jolly wedding?' Imelda, her hands clasped until the knuckles were white, could no longer contain herself.

'Sister Imelda!' Joan frowned at the nun. 'You have overstepped the mark now — you really have!'

'No, Reverend Mother — no, she hasn't. I couldn't have put it better myself.' Mr Thornton smiled. 'Well, you two. Are you too modern and up to date to make an important commitment like marriage?'

'No,' said Mary, 'we're not.'

'Well,' Joan said, 'how would it be if we arranged with Father Anderson to have a nice little wedding in our chapel? Sisters Amy and Louise could decorate it with greenery from the garden — it would be lovely and such a pleasure for us to do it all for you.'

'I'd make a lovely cake,' said Clare. 'With icing and all the trimmings.'

Mary looked at Allan and then at Sister Joan. 'I can't — I can't marry Allan in the chapel.'

'Well!' gasped Imelda. 'Why ever not?'

'Is it that you'd like to be married some-where else, dear — we wouldn't like to force you to do anything that you feel wouldn't

257

be right for you,' said Joan.

Mary's eyes were wide in her pale face as she held onto Allan's hand and said, 'I can't marry Allan in the chapel or anywhere because — because — I'm already married!'

'Oh dear, oh lumme — not another problem,' sighed Sister Imelda.

CHAPTER
TWENTY-TWO

'Beccy! Oh Beccy, what has been happening? Is this going to turn out to be an even greater muddle?' Mr Thornton ran his hands through his hair. 'Don't tell us there's a husband somewhere searching for you too. What on earth has been going on? Who is it for goodness sake? And how have you been hiding him?'

Mary took his hand. 'No, Dad — you've got it all wrong. When I said I couldn't marry Allan in the chapel, I meant that we-we're married already — to each other! Six months ago. We couldn't tell you because of all the contracts and stuff. We thought you'd be furious because it would have changed my image immediately — maybe destroyed the whole scene. So we got married quietly in a register office. Two cleaners were the witnesses. Allan continued to live in his flat and I went on staying with you two. We were happy — it seemed to be working — there was no publicity, then. . . .'

Mrs Thornton put her hands over her face and wept. 'And I always wanted — dreamed of helping you choose your wedding dress, Beccy! It was all going to be so — so beautiful!'

Sister Joan went to her and put an arm around her shoulders. 'But, my dear, love is more important than gigs, managers, dresses or big expensive ceremonies. They love one another, they're married, there's going to be a baby. What could be more beautiful than that?'

'But I wanted to decorate the church — I wanted a big hat —'

'You can have a big hat any time,' said Imelda, 'and there's nothing stopping them having Father Anderson giving them a blessing in the chapel and us cooking up a bit of a party, now is there?'

Mrs Thornton stopped sobbing. 'Yes, of course, you're right, that would be lovely if Beccy and Allan want —'

'Oh yes, Mum, and you can even have your big hat. I'll go with you to choose it. I'll get a posh frock too — will that be OK?'

'Oh, Beccy — I didn't mean to sound so shallow, it's just the shock. . . .'

Mr Thornton patted his wife's shoulder. 'You'll be all right old girl,' he said.

Joan glanced at Sister Clare who had been watching the proceedings between Mary and her parents like a spectator at a tennis match.

'More tea now, Sister, please — we're all in dire need I'm sure,' she smiled.

Sisters Amy and Louise had made the little chapel look like a woodland scene with holly and ivy and anything in the garden that — despite the cold weather and the storm — was still alive and well. Sister Imelda had coaxed the old boiler into temperamental working order so the room was cosy on the morning of Mary and Allan's blessing. Joan just couldn't get used to thinking of Mary as Rebecca. Now, very soon, they would all be together celebrating the love of these two young people. She sat alone in her usual pew in front of the altar. Yes, everything was looking beautiful. In the refectory was the wedding cake that Clare had lovingly made and decorated, along with all the edible delights she could think up. It was going to be a wonderful day. 'There'll just be a few guests,' Mary had said. 'Mum and Dad, of course, Bill Murray and his family, Len Harvey and his lad, PC Bradley and Mrs Bradley. . . .' She hadn't forgotten anyone.

Sister Clare — after holding up her hands

in horror when Mrs Thornton had suggested caterers — was fussing around declaring that she probably hadn't cooked enough and Sister Imelda was assuring her that she certainly had. Joan was grateful for a quiet moment in the chapel.

The service was to be at 3 p.m. She thought of Mary and her parents at the hotel in town, getting ready in all their finery, and Allan — who had been invited to stay up at the police house so that the tradition of not seeing the bride before the blessing could be observed — probably receiving a lecture from PC Bradley about keeping the children of today on the straight and narrow, as he spruced himself up for the ceremony. She smiled to herself, one of the comfortable things about being a nun, she thought, is that you never have to worry about what to wear. She looked at the little clock placed discreetly on the shelf of her pew. It was nearly midday. She wondered if Clare had given a thought to lunch, what with all the food she'd prepared for the reception but decided that she didn't feel very hungry anyway. She looked at the little altar. 'Please let it all go well,' she whispered.

CHAPTER
TWENTY-THREE

Mary's 'only a few people' were happily squashed together in the little chapel for the ceremony. Sister Emma had practised something not too complicated to play on the harmonium and Mary had particularly wanted the nuns to 'sing something nice in Latin, please'. Allan stood nervously in front of Father Anderson.

'They're here — they're here!' Sister Clare whispered as loudly as was polite from the door, before taking her place with her sisters.

Joan turned as Mary came in with her father. She noticed that Allan was looking too. Tears started in her eyes. There was their lost child in a long plain ivory satin dress. Her hair still ragged and urchin-like, studded with tiny fresh flowers and she carried a single red rose. What a contrast, thought Joan, to the girl in the blue jeans, anorak and wellies wearing the hat with 'I

Hate Cold Weather' embroidered on the front and a lifetime away from the girl on the poster wearing those stilt-like sandals.

'Don't she look posh!' she heard Len Harvey's lad whisper.

'Hush,' replied Len.

'She's "Gucci Foot", you know — Fred and me, she's going to give us free tickets when she gets going again. . . .'

'We all know — now, be quiet!' frowned Len.

Joan sighed with contentment, sang something special in Latin with her sisters and felt a glow of happiness.

'Doesn't it make you feel good?' whispered Sister Imelda. 'I think it must be God's jolly approval!'

'Yes, Imelda — I believe it jolly is!' replied Joan quietly.

Mrs Thornton under a satisfyingly enormous hat with a blue veil, dabbed gently at her eyes.

'Now, eat hearty everyone, there's plenty more in the kitchen.' Sister Clare bustled around the guests as if the occasion was a special gift just for her.

Joan felt a light touch on her arm. 'Reverend Mother?'

'Yes, Mr Thornton.'

'I want to thank you for — for everything,' he said quietly.

'It was lovely, wasn't it? Mary, er, Rebecca looked so very happy — so beautiful. . . .'

'That's not what I want to thank you for, dear lady. You saved my daughter's life and consequently — my grandchild. If you hadn't been there to take her in —'

'Oh please, it was nothing.' Joan tried hard not to remember that cold stormy night and being soaked to the skin.

'It was everything, Sister — everything. My wife and I — we must find a way to repay you.'

'Oh no, Mr Thornton, what we did — we did for love. That is at the heart of our vocation, to care for the wanderer. Except' — she paused and smiled — 'we don't get many of those nowadays.'

He looked at her and grinned. 'And — there's nothing you really need?'

'I-I,' she faltered. 'We can manage very well thank you.' Oh yes, she thought, there's plenty we need but we must tackle our own worries and try not to be one to anyone else.

He sighed. 'There are tarpaulins on the roof, your "jolly" boiler's on the blink and Len Harvey tells me that your old car didn't make its MOT! Money comes in dribs and drabs and quite frankly Reverend Mother, according to good Father Anderson, who I believe hasn't taken his thinking-cap off for a long while — you're in more than a bit of trouble.'

'You've been spying,' she gasped.

'No, Sister — I've at last been having a heart to heart with my daughter, Len Harvey has just told me about the car with no prompting and Father Anderson has come up with more than enough information — confidential, of course,' he grinned. 'Oh — and I know all about the think tank.'

'Well, yes, we do have a few problems.'

'Only a few?'

'No — quite a lot really,' she said honestly. 'And we've only a year to sort them out.'

'Well, Sister, we had our own think tank while we've been staying at the hotel and this is what we've come up with. I do hope you'll think its a good idea.'

'Please, Mr Thornton, tell me.' Joan sat down and indicated the chair beside her.

Mr Thornton sat down and began. 'It seems to me that you could very well fill a great need in this modern world. Look what you've done for Rebecca — she's a different girl. Relaxed and happy and with the confidence to make changes to her life and career. She found a peace here with you and the sisters that she could find nowhere else. There are many of her contemporaries out there in the fast lane who would be so grateful to have what Rebecca found here. The little guest room from which one can hear the sea may only seem like just another room to you but to someone seeking peace and rest — why, it would be a little bit of heaven. . . .'

Joan held up her hand. 'Please believe me — we've thought of doing bed and breakfast but there are so many rules and regulations, so much work would have to be done on the place — we just couldn't afford even to make a start and we haven't enough knowledge of the business side of things.'

Mr Thornton smiled. 'Well now, that's where we come in. We would be willing to stand the cost of all the repairs that need to be done and I do mean the "jolly" boiler too. You must let us at least do that for you. If you take on this new idea there'll have to be a lot of refurbishment — not so much as to spoil the old place but enough to make it more convenient to have a visitor. Oh yes, Sister — only one at a time. These people can afford such peace. We'll do all the necessary, discreet advertising and the business side — you'll just do what you do the best. Looking after someone in dire need of peace and quiet. It'll be very hard work, believe me, but the return you'll get will be more than enough to keep you all here, well — forever!'

Joan's eyes sparkled. 'If we could get more than enough, we could give the surplus to those people in the inner cities who look after the homeless, couldn't we? That would be fulfilling our vocation in a modern sort of way.'

He smiled at her and put his large hand over hers resting on the table. 'If that would make you all happy — yes, of course you can do that. We can arrange everything for you with our own advisers and accountants. It's the very least we can do.'

'I don't want to seem as if I'm discriminating,' said Joan softly, 'but we are a community of nuns and I-I would rather have — just ladies staying here, you understand?'

'Of course, dear Sister, of course. That won't present a problem at all,' he smiled.

'Then, Mr Thornton, on behalf of my Sisters and myself — I accept and thank you with all my heart.'

'You may feel differently when the builders are in, dear lady,' he laughed.

'Oh, Sister Clare will be in her element making gallons of tea.' Although she felt a little daunted at the thought of the great change this would bring to their lives, Joan felt as if a great weight had been lifted from her soul.

'Then relax and enjoy the party,' he said. 'Leave everything to us and I'll contact you soon about the details. Better tell your head office or whoever is in charge of your Order — but I'm sure they'll be delighted that the problems have been solved.'

'I've no doubt of that.' Joan was already composing — in her head — the letter to the Mother House.

'Gather round everyone — they're going to cut the cake now,' called Sister Clare. 'Dear Lord, let there be enough to go around.'

The afternoon went very quickly and so did the food, with just enough left over for supper. I shall tell the Sisters the news when all is calm again, thought Joan — when we're all in the kitchen finishing the left-overs. She smiled at the thought of their reactions. 'The redecorating — it'll be a terrible muddle,' Sister Clare would say. 'I'll be jolly glad to see that old boiler go out the door!' Sister Imelda would laugh. 'We must make quite sure our first aid facilities are up to date.' Madeline would make sure of that.

The guests left in ones and twos with the young couple standing at the door to be wished 'Good Luck', and 'Take Care', 'Long Life' and 'Every Happiness'. Mary beckoned to Joan and she went to them.

'What is it dear?' she said.

'We've got something for you — a keepsake,' said Mary. 'I want you to put it in a box with the think tank papers — just in case there's another rainy day.' She held out her hand in which there was something hidden.

Joan held out hers to receive. Mary placed her gift gently and lovingly in her palm. There were the diamond buckles from those impossible sandals.

Mary blushed. 'Don't say no — don't say anything. It's just so's you won't ever forget me,' she whispered.

'As if I ever could,' said Joan softly, as she embraced the girl. 'But Mary — it's far too important a gift — we can't possibly accept —'

'Please, Sister.' Mary smiled at Allan and in an attempt at imitating Bill Murray's country brogue, she said, 'You'd be doing me a good turn, Reverend. I'd be glad if you would dispose of them — they're surplus to my requirements now, you know.'

Joan laughed. 'Oh, Mary — I'm still going

to have to say no. Your dear father has made it possible for us to go on living here to do the work that we love. That was our greatest need. What I would like you to do, just for us if you like, is to put the buckles into a deposit box in the bank.' She pressed them into Mary's palm. 'Leave them there for the baby, you never know, he or she may have a rainy day and be glad to be helped by the money they could raise. Please, Mary, that would make us so happy — and how could we ever forget you, my dear — we've brought such changes to one another's lives.'

Mary looked into Joan's eyes. 'That's cool, Sister,' she said, 'if that'll really make you happy.'

'Yes, dear, it really would.'

Mary — or should she begin to think of her as Rebecca — smiled up at Allan. She slipped the buckles into his pocket and leaning close to him, she said softly, 'You were right, love — you said they wouldn't take them. We'll do just what Sister said and put them in the bank for the baby.'

Allan smiled at her and kissed the top of her head.

She grinned at him. 'And another thing — you'll have to give up the smoking now, you know. Sister Joan and me — we saw you that night in the garden under the apple tree. You've started the old habit again, haven't you?' she winked at Joan.

Allan grinned. 'No I haven't — I was using the little pen-light on my keyring to look at my watch. You and Sister Joan — you're not such good detectives as you thought.'

'I love you, you old dafty.' Mary kissed him on the cheek.

The nuns stood on the doorstep to wave to the couple and Mary's parents as they went down the drive and into the lane. Mary and Allan were in the Porsche and Mr and Mrs Thornton in their own car.

'Well, Imelda, we're going to miss that Porsche — 'specially you. It was a chance in a lifetime to drive that.' Joan raised her hand and waved at the cars.

'Well, Sister, I don't know if you're going to be cross but — well —'

'What is, Sister?'

'Mr Thornton wants Sister Ford.'

'But she's too old — she's got no MOT she's only worth a bit for spares.'

Imelda reddened. 'Yes, I know — but you see, when I went with them to get Mary's car out of the barn, he saw Sister Ford. You've never seen anything like it, Mother — he was almost in tears. You see, it's exactly like the car that they used to come down here for holidays in. He wanted to buy it there and then. I said that it was past it and not worth a bean. But he said please — ever so nicely' — she blushed — 'so I said yes — but that he could have it for nothing.'

'Very well done, Imelda.' Joan smiled.

'Well, it seems that, after all, it won't be for nothing. You see, he's coming to get it tomorrow with Len Harvey, and I don't know if you noticed, but I did — in Len's showroom there was one of those seven-seater people carriers. He wants to swap us that for Sister Ford! Oh please don't be angry, Mother — but I said yes!'

Joan took her hand and sighed. 'Imelda, I'm too tired and amazed to be angry. I've spent so much time worrying about things and trying to find solutions for everything I almost forgot that there's Someone watching all the time who has all the answers.'

Mary's car stopped just at their side of the iron gates and the girl leaned out to wave goodbye. 'We'll be in touch — after the scan — tell you if it's a girl or a boy,' she called. 'Thank you for everything. See ya soon! Maybe Christmas!'

The car moved off and down the lane. The sisters watched until it went round a bend and out of sight.

'Well!' said Sister Imelda, 'that's that then!'

Sister Joan, her hand still raised in farewell, said, 'Yes, and what a change that child has made in our lives — who would have guessed.' She adjusted her veil before lowering her hand slowly to her side, dashing away a tear before the others noticed.

'She'll be OK now,' said Clare and patted her shoulder kindly. 'All settled nicely.'

'It's all so — so romantic,' said young Sister Emma. 'But it'll be nice to be quiet again for a while. I suppose we'll never know where she hid her wedding ring all this time.'

Joan realized with surprise that she hadn't thought about that. So Mary, she smiled to herself, you take a little mystery away with you.

Sister Flora put her hand on Joan's arm. 'Mrs Thornton said she'd pay for me to have a false tooth — Mary told her all about it, you see — but I said no thank you. I'm managing very well without.' Her smile revealed an endearing gap.

The house seemed so still. The wind was blowing cold around the front porch and Joan felt that she'd be glad to go indoors and sit by the fire for a while. She watched as the wind blew the last of the fallen leaves across the drive. The old dead oak was no more than firewood now, piled high on the other side of the gates. They would have plenty of yule logs for a warm Christmas. The lane was empty but the days ahead would be full and busy. It's going to be hard work, she thought, but we're all used to that. She thought of Mary and Allan driving back into the world eager to begin a life together with their baby. She smiled to herself. You'll be fine, Rebecca Marie, she thought, you're young, strong and you have love in your heart and your life. You'll learn to be brave, and as for the future, well — who knows, Mary Winter — who knows!

We hope you have enjoyed this Large Print book. Other Thorndike, Wheeler, Kennebec, and Chivers Press Large Print books are available at your library or directly from the publishers.

For information about current and upcoming titles, please call or write, without obligation, to:

Publisher
Thorndike Press
295 Kennedy Memorial Drive
Waterville, ME 04901
Tel. (800) 223-1244

or visit our Web site at:

http://gale.cengage.com/thorndike

OR

Chivers Large Print
published by BBC Audiobooks Ltd
St James House, The Square
Lower Bristol Road
Bath BA2 3SB
England
Tel. +44(0) 800 136919
email: bbcaudiobooks@bbc.co.uk
www.bbcaudiobooks.co.uk

All our Large Print titles are designed for easy reading, and all our books are made to last.